# CONVICTION

Other titles by S. Usher Evans

## THE DEMON SPRING TRILOGY

Resurgence

Revival

Redemption

## THE MADION WAR TRILOGY

The Island

The Chasm

The Union

## THE LEXIE CARRIGAN CHRONICLES

Spells and Sorcery

Magic and Mayhem

Dawn and Devilry

Illusion and Indemnity

## THE PRINCESS VIGILANTE SERIES

The City of Veils

The Veil of Ashes

The Veil of Trust

The Queen of Veils

# CONVICTION

## THE RAZIA SERIES
## BOOK 3

S. Usher Evans

Sun's Golden Ray
Publishing

Line-editing by Regina West


ISBN: 1945438010
ISBN-13: 978-1945438011

## THE RAZIA SERIES

Double Life
Alliances
Conviction
Fusion

Beginnings, a Razia Novella
The Razia Short Story Collection

# DEDICATION

To Bex and Kristin
My first and most trusted beta readers
I wouldn't be here if not for you

# CHAPTER ONE

Lyssa Peate was dying.

Literally, she was dying of boredom and misery and if she sat in this small room for one more second, her soul would be leached out of her and sent to Leveman's Vortex.

"*Herbre twings wriffels*," the purple man said, making about as much sense as he'd made the three weeks they'd been in this terrible mess.

At the front of the room sat the representative from the Planetary and System Science Academy Department for Inclusionary Investigation, a tall, sinewy man with a halo of hair around his bald scalp. "Honestly, can we get a translator or something?"

His assistant, a mustachioed man with a thick accent,

flipped through his paperwork. "Sir, as we've not yet translated their language, there are none."

"Not even a close cousin?"

Lyssa was a twenty-two-year-old, planet-discovering scientist known as a Deep Space Explorer. She was in the middle of a planetary excavation—documenting the biological and chemical makeup of a planet for the purposes of selling it—when she stumbled upon a village of these sentient creatures. Ten feet tall with purple scaly skin, the creatures came in peace, curious about the young woman who had appeared out of nowhere.

"Well, get them a pen or something."

Per the Academy regulations, any planet with a population meeting the five standards for intelligent life would be considered for inclusion into the Universal Beings Union, the unwieldy and sparse universal government alliance. The process was long and painful, made more difficult by the initial work to even understand the creatures.

"God in Leveman's, Czappa, show the poor thing how to hold it."

Until its UBU status was determined, the planet remained in limbo. If the planet were included, then there would be no sale, and Lyssa would be compensated for her trouble. But until that determination was made, Lyssa remained the owner of the planet. And as the planet's representative, she was forced to sit in these inane meetings.

"Yes, that's it. Now like this." The Inclusionary Investigation representative gestured like he was drawing something in the air. The purple man gave him a look that required no translation.

Most scientists had assistants or interns for this sort of thing. But Lyssa was an island unto herself and decided she didn't want anyone's help. She was simply skating by, doing the minimum possible amount of work to stay under the radar and still make enough money to cover her other life as a space pirate bounty hunter named Razia.

Her head lolled and she looked down at the paper in front of her where she had written a list of fifty names. They were the recorded identities of every pirate sitting at a random bar on the planet D-882. As a bounty hunter, she was given access to the Universal Bank and all the transaction data recorded any time someone slid their C-card to pay for something. Each of the fifty names on her list had purchased a drink in the past hour, and Lyssa had been passing the time by investigating each one to see if any could be one of the most wanted pirates in the universe. Or at least, she was until her mini-computer battery died.

"Yes, look, he's doing it."

In any case, most of the names that she'd come across were duds—low-level criminals that weren't worth her time. But her haphazard process had netted a new alias for Linro Lee, a member of a rival pirate web.

"I don't understand what he just wrote. Is that some kind of language?"

She was feeling the pressure to capture more pirates than usual, hoping to regain some favor with her own runner, Dissident. He was none-too-pleased with her for getting wrapped up in the presidential assassination a few months prior and downright pissed that she had interrupted his easy funding stream.

Lyssa scowled and resisted the urge to roll her eyes. It wasn't *her* fault she got wrapped up in that mess. Lizbeth Carter had all but blackmailed her into tagging along and helping to uncover the conspiracy. Although Lizbeth was now the closest thing Lyssa had to a best friend, Lizbeth had still made Lyssa's membership in Dissident's web even more tenuous than it had been, even as the seventeenth most wanted pirate.

Normal bounty hunters had many small bounties on their own heads, a few thousand here, ten thousand there. These bounties were usually funded by the runners in other pirate webs, eager to see a particularly active bounty hunter knocked down a few pegs. In a rather twisted way, it was almost a sign of respect. And since nobody respected Razia, nobody put any money on her.

Her dirty secret was that the credits behind her bounty came not from another pirate, but her old Academy boss, Pymus, who was trying to blackmail her. Although Pymus was currently enjoying his stay at the bottom of a fiery river in Leveman's Vortex, Lyssa had other problems. His bounty was going to expire soon, and with it went her standing in the top twenty.

She blew air through her lips, catching the attention of the man to her left. She glared at him and he turned back to the meeting.

"I think he just wrote down something. Can you...no, we don't have any translators."

Razia's strategy to rectify her situation was simple: get out and capture as many pirates as she possibly could. If they didn't respect her, perhaps they'd just add to her bounty on her to get her to go away. Unfortunately, that great plan had been derailed with the discovery of this planet.

She glowered out towards the meeting, where they were no closer to translating the purple aliens' language than when they started a month ago. She was wasting precious time, and the longer she sat there, the more it grated on her. In-between looking up bounties, Lyssa had been tossing ideas back and forth electronically with Lizbeth on ways to get out of the meeting (she had gotten so desperate as to offer to cut off her own finger).

"Yes boy, what is it?"

"Pardon me, but I have an urgent message from Dr. Peate's supervisor that cannot wait."

Lyssa's head shot up at the familiar voice. Her eyes scanned the room until they landed on him—her savior. Seventeen years old with a meticulous part down the left side of his blond head, her little brother Vel was a most welcome sight. His expression was a mixture of sycophantic deference with an underlying amusement that Lyssa was sure only she saw.

"Oh, er, very well then, we shall complete this another time," said the man at the head of the table. He turned to Lyssa with a most pompous expression. "We will need you or your representative here at all times—"

Lyssa didn't even hear the end of his sentence, as she had bounded out the door with Vel in tow.

"God in Leveman's Vortex," Lyssa gasped, as if he had saved her from drowning. "You are the best. I can't even...so thankful that you—"

"You're quite welcome, Lyssa."

She shifted, giving Vel a look that communicated how she felt about being lured her out of one horrible situation and into another. Used to Lyssa's mood swings, Vel simply smiled back at her.

"What do you want, Dorst?" she said.

"Many things. Starting with a little respect from my subordinate."

She rolled her eyes and turned to him. Dorst was the second oldest of the twenty-four Peates. He, like Vel and most of the brood, shared their mother's light hair and fine expression.

Lyssa's eyes shifted to the man next to Dorst who looked awfully familiar. She blinked; he wasn't familiar, per se, but standing next to Dorst and Vel, he resembled them mightily.

"Who's this?" Lyssa said, folding her arms over her chest.

"You *brat*," the unknown man snapped. "I'm your brother!"

Lyssa shrugged and could not believe he expected her to recognize him. In the first place, she preferred to believe her family didn't exist (and most of them felt the same about her). And in the second, twenty-four names and faces were a lot to remember. The only ones she could recall with easy clarity were Vel, Dorst (because he was her supervisor), Sera (her despised eldest sister), and...Jukin.

"And your name is...?" she drawled.

"*Heelin*!" he croaked. "God in Leveman's Vortex, Lyssa, I sat right in front of you in classes for five years and you don't even remember my name?"

"Oh..." She wasn't actually ashamed; she'd spent most of her Academy education glued to her mini-computer looking up bounties for Tauron, or hunting for Tauron himself. Somewhere in the back of her memory, she might have remembered having a brother in class with her, but since they all hated her, she didn't really care.

Heelin folded his arms over his chest petulantly and scowled at Dorst. "I'm not working for *her*."

"Wait, what?" Lyssa gasped, visions of the last internship dancing in her mind. On the whole, it had turned out all right, but she couldn't risk another brother knowing her secret. "I'm sorry," she found herself repeating. "I can't take on another intern."

"*I'm older than you*!"

She jumped at Heelin's ferocity; she was normally the one doing the yelling.

"So..." she said, looking to Dorst who looked far too amused for the ire he had caused.

"I am *assigning*," Dorst gave Heelin a look that could kill, "Heelin to work with you for a while. Take on some of your workload."

"Why?" she deadpanned.

"Well, you've got other things to be getting on with other than this business on your planet, right?" Dorst said, motioning to the meeting room. "Heelin will take over. It will be maturing for him to spend some time out of the field and in the Academy."

Lyssa began to chuckle as Heelin's face reddened. This was punishment, pure and simple. "What'd you do, Heelin?"

"That's none of your business," Dorst interjected. "What is your business is that I expect you to mentor Heelin."

"*What?*" came the response in unison.

"Lyssa, you have been running around here like a one woman show for years now—don't interrupt," Dorst snapped as she opened her mouth. "It's time you learn how to work with other people."

"I know how to work with other people," Lyssa huffed.

Dorst smiled at her. "Name one person that you've worked with in the past six months."

She opened her mouth to speak and then closed it abruptly. Lyssa Peate hadn't been working with Lizbeth on the plot to uncover the assassination attempt of the president, the news organization named the space pirate Razia as her partner. Although more people than she preferred knew about her double lives, Dorst was not one of them.

She tossed a look to Vel, but he simply cleared his throat. "Lyssa, I agree with Dorst."

"Get sucked," she snapped. "You always take his side!"

"Oh, and Lyss," Dorst said, ignoring the way she bristled at him, "when you get a moment, stop in. We need to discuss some things with your career." With that, he turned and walked the way he came.

She glowered at Dorst's retreating back. "I'ma stop in and take you to see the last supervisor I had..."

"Oh, you know he'd make it through to the Arch." Vel

was smiling at her in the annoyingly pleasant way he did when he was smug about something.

"You are a traitorous bastard," Lyssa growled.

"I thought he could keep you company," Vel said, nodding to Heelin, who was similarly growling about this injustice.

"C-company?" Lyssa prayed Vel hadn't divulged her secret. Far too many people knew about that now, thanks to Lizbeth's blabbering to the crew of Sage Teon, the only pirate who actually gave a damn about her.

"Yes, as I'm about to leave for my planetary survival course," Vel said, as if they'd had this discussion multiple times already.

"Oh God in…that's today?" Lyssa whipped out her mini-computer to check the date, but it was still dead. The planetary survival course was a rite of passage for all DSE candidates. Three months alone on a planet with whatever the candidate thought to bring with them.

"Yeah, so," Vel said, shifting uncomfortably. "I'll see you in about three months?"

"Want me to come get you?" Lyssa asked.

"You can't go get him," Heelin drawled. "It's not allowed —"

"Heelin, the amount of care that I have about that statement is minuscule," Lyssa snapped before turning to Vel. "Seriously, I can—"

"Lyssa, it's okay. I'm actually looking forward to…well, to being alone for a while."

"Oh yeah, how's that girlfriend of yours?"

Vel's face faltered. "Lyssa, I told you that I broke up with her last week."

Lyssa winced. "Sorry, been wrapped up with this whole…"

"No, I get it." Vel smiled, but she noticed it didn't quite reach his eyes.

She shifted uncomfortably, "So…do you have time for a quick lunch before—"

"No, sorry," Vel said, sounding genuinely so. "The shuttle leaves in about half an hour."

Lyssa felt bad that she'd forgotten something so important in Vel's life. "Want me to walk you there?"

"Why don't you two take a chance to…uh…get reacquainted." Vel nodded to Heelin who looked like he had something terrible under his nose.

"You know this is nothing but another lame attempt to get me to tell Dorst about Sostas, right?" Lyssa hissed.

"Of course, because when's the last time Dorst asked about Father?"

She had no response; it had been some time.

Vel pulled her into a hug. "I'll miss ya, Lyss."

She awkwardly returned the hug, leaning into him a bit. She couldn't help but feel like they were growing apart now, him off into Academy career and her into…whatever she was doing with her double lives. She rather envied him for his focus on what he wanted.

"Go catch a bunch of pirates for me," he whispered so only she could hear.

And just like that, he broke free and left her standing

alone in the middle of the hall. Watching him go felt almost as terrible as when she'd woken up and saw Sostas' ship flying away for the last time.

Heelin's drawling sneer broke her reverie. "Are you just going to stand here all day?"

She studied him for a second, making sure to notice all of the ways he was just like the rest of the Peates. They were all the same, save Vel. "You aren't going to find anything out."

"About *what*?"

"Sostas."

"I'm sure I don't care about Father's secrets," Heelin retorted. "The man left, who cares? Half of my professors thought he was a nutjob anyways."

Lyssa felt the urge to deck Heelin, but resisted it. Dorst might write her up for attacking a fellow scientist, especially one who was supposed to be her employee.

Heelin crossed his arms and glared at her. "So what am I supposed to do for you, huh? Sit in a meeting for you while you go do…Leveman's knows what?"

Her eyes widened.

"Is that what Dorst told you to do?" she asked, a bit breathlessly.

Heelin rolled his eyes again, and she wondered if they would permanently stick up there. "He said I'm to take over your Inclusionary Investigation."

"You are, huh?" If the investigation dragged on for weeks —months—that could give her ample time to spend on D-882. They required DSEs to excavate and sell a minimum of three planets per quarter, but since she was entangled in this sentient creature mire, they had given her a waiver until it was resolved. She wouldn't have to set foot on the Academy for…well, for however long it would take them to work through the bureaucracy.

Without the need to return back to the Academy, she could round up every single one of the top twenty.

Then the other pirates would *have* to notice her.

She glanced down the hall to where Vel had disappeared and felt a surge of affection for her little brother. Perhaps this was his plan all along!

"What are you grinning about?" Heelin said with a scowl.

"My dear Heelin," Lyssa said, rubbing her hands together in glee, "so, the deal is you work for me right?"

He grimaced painfully but did not correct her.

"So, in that case, *you* will stay here, in this room, with these…things," Lyssa ordered. "You will represent me in all Academy meetings. You will write up whatever reports they want—"

"But—"

"That's what Dorst said, right?" Lyssa continued with a devilish grin. "You work for me now. This is what I'm directing you to do."

"I thought *you* were supposed to be learning how to work with other people?" Heelin asked.

"I am going to work with other people. I'm going to work with them right over to the bounty office…"

"What was that?"

"Nothing!"

***

Perched on the edge of a plastic bench on the notoriously unreliable pirate transport system, Razia, now dressed in her cargo pants and black boots, was headed into heart of the pirate city on the planet D-882. She couldn't help the grin that seemed permanently etched on her face. She hadn't been this happy in weeks, months, maybe even years.

She giggled loudly, drawing the attention of two men sitting on the opposite side of the shuttle. She'd taken care to find the cheapest possible docking station on D-882, even farther out than usual, since she was planning to be there for a long time. She giggled again, then cleared her throat when the two men glared at her. She made sure to return their stares with gusto as she departed the car.

The transport shuttle was operated by the four pirate runners, which was why it rarely worked. Case in point: the escalator that normally carried her up to the top level was out of order, meaning she had to climb up at least three stories' worth of stairs. Even as her quads burned, nothing could dampen her mood as she emerged into the blinding heat of the desert city

She sauntered into a bar directly across from the station, catching the attention of the middle-aged man in a booth who watched her with a mix of curiosity and adoration. Harms was her pirate informant, a man that knew practically everything about everything in the pirate universe. Although he was supposed to be impartial to the four webs, he had something of a soft spot for Razia.

"Why are you so happy?" he asked, looking her up and down.

"I..." Razia's mind drew a blank for a fake reason for her good mood. Just as Dorst didn't know about Lyssa's life as Razia, Harms didn't know about Razia's life as Lyssa Peate. "I just am," she said finally.

"Okay, keep your secrets." Harms sat back as a serving robot placed a glass of water in front of him. "To what do I owe the pleasure of your company?"

"Well, I wanted to know if you'd heard anyone talking about me?"

Harms took a sip of his water. "Yep."

"I mean...anything good."

"No, honey." Harms shook his head. "Everyone is still pretty pissed off at you."

"Yeah, I figured." Razia slumped down in the booth, then shook her head and sat back up again. Now was not the time to be defeated. "Okay, so, next question: Who does everyone want captured?"

"Oh." Harms scratched his graying beard. "Relleck probably."

Razia winced and tried to hide it. Her whatever with Relleck was another thing Harms didn't know about. "Who else?"

"You."

Razia growled. "Who else?"

"Sage."

"Harms, for crying out loud, I'm trying to get noticed here!" To his amused face, she added, "Positively."

"What are you so worried about?" Harms asked. "You're still seventeenth."

"Until my bounty expires. Which could be any day now."

"It's only been a year."

"And it hasn't changed a single credit! Which means that when it expires—it's going to expire—then I'll be at zero." Her good mood evaporated. "*Normal* bounty hunters don't have to work this hard. *Normal* bounty hunters who've captured almost every one in the top twenty get money on their heads. *Normal* bounty hunters—"

"Are dudes," Harms said gently. She puffed up and he held up his hands in defense. "I'm not saying it's right. I'm just saying it's the truth. And now, with all of this presidential mumbo jumbo hanging over your head, it's just not the right time to try and win people over."

"There *is* no right time," she said darkly.

"I know you didn't just come here to complain," Harms said, sipping his water. "What's cooking in that brain of yours?"

She graciously accepted the topic change. Harms' patience with her was not unlimited. "It looks like I'm going to be here for a while, so I was going to try and pick off the top twenty in succession. Make a big show of it."

She glanced up at Harms to gauge his reaction. He seemed unimpressed, but he also didn't look like he hated the idea.

"Worth a shot," he said after a moment. "Eli Stenson just dipped out of the top ten, so Dissident doesn't have anyone up there right now. He seems to be in a bad mood about it, too."

Razia brightened. "So he might not be so angry if I knock

off everyone's top pirates?"

"There's a reason why these guys are the most wanted. Most of them have been there for a while. It's been a long time since we've had a fluke show up, so don't do anything stupid."

"I'm *not* going to do anything *stupid*."

Harms ignored her bristling. "You say that, and yet you've got that crazy look in your eye."

After about an hour of discussion about the ninth and tenth most wanted pirates in the universe (and a payment of about half a million credits), Razia was on her way to hunting Gunnar Bodhi and Jarvis Loeb. She added the information she'd gleaned from Harms to what she'd already uncovered—

Someone grabbed her by the arm and yanked her into an alleyway. Before she had time to react, almost-familiar lips pressed against hers. And along with them, she tasted smoke and booze and retched in disgust.

She pushed him away. "I told you not to smoke before you do this."

"Aw, come on," Relleck said with a grin, "you like it."

"No, I don't," she said, backing up from him, but he kissed her again. Sensing that her disgust wasn't enough to dissuade him, she tried a different tactic. She pulled away and hissed, "Someone could see you."

He stepped back and she scowled at the taste still in her mouth. She still wasn't used to this. Whatever they were doing it was strange and weird and just wrong. Razia didn't want to know what Dissident would say if he found out she was fraternizing with the enemy.

Besides, even after two months, she still hadn't even let Relleck see her ship. She definitely didn't trust him beyond these back alley make-out sessions.

"What are you even doing here?" Razia asked, crossing her arms over her chest.

"You hear about this Pirate Ball thing?"

Razia heard pirate ball and thought of only one thing. "What in Leveman's Vortex is a pirate ball?"

"The runners wanna celebrate the Piracy Act. It's been twenty years," Relleck said, slid his hands along her back. "So they're making us all get dressed up in tuxes and come to Eamon's."

Razia couldn't help her barking laughter when she thought of someone like Sage Teon, one of her other pirate friends, in a tuxedo. It was laughable.

"Yeah, well, that sounds like a riot." Razia rolled her eyes. "You idiots have fun."

"Contestant's making all of us go to it—wants to show up the rest of the runners." Relleck glanced at the ground, strangely nervous. "You wanna go with me?"

Razia stared at him, her brain trying to comprehend the words that floated in the air. Being with Relleck, his hands on her back, the disgusting taste of smoke and him on her lips, and now he was…asking her…out?

"What…like as your date?" The word sounded absolutely ridiculous in her head.

"Yeah, why not?"

"Because first of all, this"—she pointed between the two of them—"isn't that. I don't want everyone knowing that we're...whatever."

"What, so you'd rather go with Sage Teon?"

She blinked. "Sage?"

"Yeah, you two are always talking." He sniffed and leaned against the wall. "What's going on between you?"

"Um...he's my..." she thought for a moment, wondering how to define him before realizing that was just stupid. "He's whatever. I just don't want to go. Period." She paused for effect. "I don't wear dresses."

"But I would love to see you in a dress," Relleck said, pulling her into his arms and she gagged at the smell of him. "Actually, I'd love to see you in nothing—" And he was kissing her again, passionately, and in such a way that made her breathless and wonder if she should let him onto her ship. But she couldn't relax; it still felt weird when he tried to be affectionate towards her. Especially now, when all she could think about were the frilly dresses at the balls her mother used to throw.

She roughly pushed him away. "I can't do this right now."

"You never can do this any time," Relleck huffed. "What are you even doing?"

"I'm working," Razia said evasively. Relleck had been tangentially involved with the Pymus fiasco and her bounty, and she wasn't eager to discuss the subject in depth.

Relleck was too self-absorbed to notice her worry, as he whined loudly, "So you would rather work than spend time with me?"

Razia pursed her lips and stuck her hand on her hip. "You

sound like a girl."

"Well, one of us should, I guess," he muttered. Razia wondered why that hurt a little bit. Maybe Lizbeth had rubbed off on her. "Can you at least tell me where in Leveman's you've been over the past month?"

She cocked her head to the side. "Was out of the area taking care of business."

"What kind of—"

"Why do you want to know?" She finally stepped back from him and narrowed her eyes.

"Because..." he trailed off, and she filled in her own blanks.

"Exactly," she said, pushing him off of her.

"I'm trying, Razia," he said, pulling her back in, "but you're making it so damn difficult to figure you out." He tucked a strand of hair behind her ear, and she didn't like the intimate touch. "What are you so afraid of?"

She stepped back from him. "I'm not afraid of anything."

"Clearly." He rolled his eyes and let her go. "Look, if you want to go to the party with me, hit me up."

Razia watched him leave the alley. She was perplexed and confused, as she usually was when they parted. He was as much a stranger now as before they'd added the physical aspect to things.

But Relleck was a conundrum for another day. She had work to do and pirates to impress.

Without another word, she turned around and began walking towards her first quarry.

# CHAPTER TWO

Gunnar Bodhi was an easy capture. She stalked the tenth most wanted pirate for only two days before he made a mistake, drinking too much and then leaving with a girl instead of his burly body men. Razia brought him to the bounty office before he even knew what hit him. She made sure that everyone else in line at the bounty office knew that she had a top-ten bounty.

But predictably, when faced with *actual* proof of her abilities as a bounty hunter, they opted to just ignore her.

The moment she left the bounty office, she was already on the heels of her next target, Jarvis Loeb. He was the ninth most wanted pirate and the difference between him and Bodhi was night and day.

After the first week, she knew everything there was to know about this pirate. He'd been in Protestor's web for fifteen years and was primarily interested in hijacking ships, though he'd dabbled a bit in bounty hunting. What made him such a different sort of pirate is that he was a teetotaler and went to Temple (where the faithful worshipped the Great Creator at Leveman's Vortex) at least once a week if not more.

Razia knew there was one small house of worship on D-882, but after spending a week trailing Loeb, she was now more acquainted with it than the Temple at the Manor where she grew up.

She snorted; not as if she'd spent much time there either.

She sighed and checked the time on her mini-computer. It had been an hour since he'd gone inside for services, so he would be coming out any time now.

She sat back and took in the sight of the small Temple, crammed between a bar and a cathouse. It was barely recognizable as a house of worship, with a nondescript door and a hanging light out front. Only the small etching of Leveman's Vortex distinguished it from the rest of the buildings.

She'd been there once before, when Vel was still her intern. He hadn't believed her when she told him there was one on the planet, so she'd brought him there to prove it. It still amazed her that Vel adhered to the whole "organized religion" thing, especially since they'd come face to face with the real deal. He'd explained once that he found *comfort* in the predictability of the religion. Thanks to her childhood priest constantly informing her she was a bad soul, she'd never found comfort in anything related to Temple.

She did miss Vel's presence, especially now that he was out of range for the next three months. She wondered how he was doing alone on that planet by himself. He seemed awfully needy of human contact, after all. Being alone for that long might kill him.

Without another thought, she fired off a quick message to Lizbeth, wondering what the investigator was doing. A few moments passed with no response. Razia sighed and kicked the ground absent-mindedly.

She looked at her mini-computer and considered messaging Relleck, but then he might expect more than just kissing. And as much as the idea of that excited her, at the same time, it was a bit nauseating.

He'd asked her out to the *Pirate Ball* of all things. Razia heard more about it from Harms when she'd stopped in a few days ago, but it still didn't sound like anything Razia wanted to do. She recalled with vivid and disgusting clarity how the pirates stared at her mini-skirt during her ill-fated infiltration of their secret meeting. They would just *love* an excuse to leer at her again.

Then again, she'd also taken to wearing a little eyeliner. And the idea of a dress, of looking pretty and feeling as good as when Lizbeth put makeup on her, was kind of tempting. It wasn't an everyday thing, of course (she scoffed at the idea), but once in a while, to be the pretty girl…

She tamped down that idea quickly, refocusing her rambling thoughts back to the problem at hand. She could be pretty and girly, or as much as she could stomach, when someone put a bounty on her head. Until then, she needed to keep her nose to the grindstone.

As if proving her point, the doors to the temple opened finally and a few patrons came pouring out, Loeb and his two giant guards included.

She scowled and slunk back into the alley. So much for that plan.

***

Another two days passed, and Razia was starting to get pissed off. She'd *never* had this much trouble cornering a bounty. She actually went inside for a Temple sermon, just to see if there was a chance she could get Loeb alone, but his bodyguards sat nearby, and all she got was a reminder about how the Great Creator was keen on damning wayward souls to Plethegon.

She walked out into the late afternoon sun and let the memories of childhood settle on top of her before considering her next move. She was so lost in thought that she walked right by the U-POL officer whose uniform was flecked with gold.

"Hands up, *pirate*."

She stopped mid-stride and groaned. The officer, Opli, was one of the Universal Police's Special Forces, the elite group charged with eradicating piracy and led by none other than Lyssa's own brother Jukin. Thanks to Dissident and the other runners, all the Special Forces were allowed to do was march around D-882 and check identification.

"Oh, come on, junior, you know this is futile," she

scoffed.

"ID, please," Opli said with the ferocity of someone who could actually arrest her. She rolled her eyes and made a big show of comparing her two IDs. Having multiple aliases was expressly illegal per the UBU, and also one of the main ways pirates stayed hidden from bounty hunters. Though Opli had no idea that her other ID said Lyssandra Peate, she could still flaunt her disrespect for his rules in his face.

"Just want to make sure I'm giving you the right one," she said, eyeing the two side-by-side, making sure to hide the name on her Lyssa Peate ID. "Here you go, champ."

Opli snatched her card away and swiped it in his handheld reader. She added an extra layer of obnoxious indignation as she waited. She knew he knew who she (Razia) was. He'd been there when she and Lizbeth prevented the assassination. He'd been there with General State let them both out, overriding Jukin and Opli's protests.

Razia cocked her head to the side and wondered if Opli knew about just how far his idol had attempted to go. Jukin, the self-proclaimed bastion of moral superiority, was not only complicit in the assassination attempt, but also planned to blame pirates for it. When the plot was discovered, Jukin was a hair's breadth away from ruined, if not for Razia. For some reason, she'd felt compelled to save his ass.

"What are you looking at?" Opli snarled, almost throwing her C-card back at her.

"Just thinking about how awesome it was to save the UBU a few months ago." His face reddened and she smirked. "Remember when you had to let me out of jail? Bet that absolutely killed you."

"I remember that your little girlfriend was assisting a known pirate," Opli shot back. "And if you aren't careful, I might just take a trip to S-864 and arrest her for violation of the Piracy Act, as *she's* not covered by your stupid laws."

Razia narrowed her eyes at him and bared her teeth. "Yeah, and if you lay a finger on one of her golden curls, I will end you and your stupid boss. Slowly, painfully, and totally."

Opli snarled back, and for a moment, she wondered which of them would break first. She certainly had nothing else to do than stand there and glare at her mortal enemy, but Opli apparently had other priorities. He stepped back, looking annoyed to have done so, turned on his heel and stormed off.

She watched him go with an empty sort of satisfaction, still picturing his face if she had handed him Lyssa Peate's ID card. She mostly kept the two lives separate because her DSE funds allowed her an untraceable source of income, allowing her to move around without being spotted by other bounty hunters.

That is, if other bounty hunters actually *wanted* to spot her.

That nasty little thought brought her back down to reality and she grimaced, checking her own bounty again to see if it had changed in the last five minutes.

It hadn't, just as it hadn't in over a year.

She grumbled and stuffed her hands in her pockets, as she ran through a thousand scenarios for how she could entrap

Jarvis Loeb.

***

"Another one, darlin'?" The young waitress at Eamon's paused by Razia's table. The other woman's shorts were barely covering her butt, long tan legs filling a pair of sky-high heels that would make even Lizbeth cringe in pain.

"Yeah," Razia grunted, pushing her empty glass towards her.

It had been three weeks, and Razia was as close to capturing Jarvis Loeb as Dissident was to adopting her. Loeb was also apparently in a committed relationship and wasn't prone to spending the night with loose women. So all of the usual methods for capturing a pirate were, in effect, out the window. No matter what creative solution Razia came up with, there seemed to be no way to get past Loeb's mammoth bodyguards.

Razia continued to pursue him out of pure stubbornness. Somewhere in the back of her mind, she knew that she might have been smarter to let this one go and find someone else. But she couldn't, and every day she grew more and more irrationally attached to the idea. The only way she could quiet the grinding thoughts was to drown them in suds.

Besides, Lizbeth was always crowing that Razia worked too hard (which was rich, coming from Miss-I'm-Too-Busy-With-A-Government-Investigation-To-See-You). At least the next time they spoke, Razia could shove it in her face that she took a night off.

Razia had to threaten her way in the back door, as she was still technically banned from when she had discovered the top pirate watering hole was really an elaborate ruse to discover secret aliases for pirates. But Eamon's was still the place to be seen. Glancing around the bar, Razia counted no less than ten of the most well-known pirates—Conboy Conrad and Max Fried, along with Eli Stentson and some others from Dissident's web.

Sliding her mini-computer over to herself, she refreshed the transaction history of the bar, hoping a little game of "who's who" would amuse her and maybe turn up an unknown alias.

| Eamon's | | |
|---|---|---|
| Time of Transaction | Account | Amount |
| UT20015-08–10-90:45 | Henry, Samuel | 15C |

She glanced up at the terminal and spied Arpad Bernal, a member of Contestant's web. But she knew she'd see him there as this alias wasn't hidden.

| Eamon's | | |
|---|---|---|
| Time of Transaction | Account | Amount |
| UT20015-08–10-90:47 | Diesel, Ky | 15C |

She didn't recognize the guy, but saw him walk over to Waslow Needler. That figured, she supposed. While Ky wasn't a top pirate, he was on Needler's crew. And crews always got in on their boss's dime.

| Eamon's | | |
|---|---|---|
| Time of Transaction | Account | Amount |
| UT20015-08–10-90:49 | Leon, Jamison | 50C |

She grimaced and slunk lower in the booth to delay the inevitable. That was Sage's very first alias, which he continued to use even after she'd pointed out how close the last name (Leon) was to his own name (Teon). But if he was there, that meant he brought his crew as well, and so it was only a matter of time before…

"Hey gorgeous!"

The voice belonged to the generally most obnoxious man Razia had ever come into contact with, Ganon, Sage's pilot. His voice echoed across the room as only his could, and he nearly skipped over to her table. She hissed at him to go away, but he ignored her completely and sat down in the booth next to her.

"Drinking alone looks good on no one, babe," Ganon said with a impish wink that enraged her. He stood up in the booth and waved to catch the attention of the rest of the crew. One by one, they appeared at the booth and sat down: Sobal, the young computer hacker, Keal, the mechanic, and the three giant bodyguards, crowding her uncomfortably into the small space of the booth.

Then finally, the last of the motley crew appeared, three pitchers of beer in his hands. Sage's eyes settled on Razia and his face lit up. He was a year or two older than Razia. She'd known for as long as she'd been a pirate and begrudgingly accepted him as helpful at times. He was such an insufferable asshole that whatever positive virtues he had were drowned out.

As to prove his point, he ordered the men in the booth out with a flick of his head, and slid in next to Razia before she could make her escape. The rest of the crew filed back in, effectively trapping her.

"There now, are we all comfortable?" Sage said, sliding the pitchers of beer around. "Enjoy."

"Thanks, boss!" came the chorus of replies as the men went to town on the pitchers. Sage sat back and watched the melee; the pitchers were gone in a matter of moments. Even Razia's beer was refilled, thanks to Ganon.

"Ah," Sage said, leaning back into the booth. "Happy crew, happy boss."

Razia snorted and drank some of her beer. She was a little buzzed, enough to support civilized conversation with Sage and his crew.

"So what did you do?" she asked, licking foam off of her lip.

"Oh, the guys and I just finished a couple million credit job," Sage said as if it were all in a day's work. "Real fine work, gents. Truly a sight to behold."

Razia nodded; that was about as much interest as her current state of inebriation would allow. She zoned out, feigning a nod and a smile when needed, while he described his conquest.

"Pretty cool, huh?" Sage grinned at her.

"Yep," she said. Her beer went from half-filled to full again.

"You've been hanging out on'882 a lot lately."

Her head spun around. "You been watching me?"

"Harms said you've been by a bunch lately," Sage said with a small cough. "You done with that scientist stuff or what?"

She smirked. "Actually, I got someone to cover for me for a while."

"Oh?"

"Yeah, get this," she said with a slight slur, "so, I got an *employee* now."

"Poor guy." Sage laughed. "Did you leave him on a planet, too?"

"Get sucked. Vel was...eventually fine," Razia hissed at him. Before Vel knew her secret, she "accidentally" forgot him on a planet for a few days.

"And so you've been playing pirate while he's covering for you?"

She scowled. "I am not *playing pirate*."

"Well, what have you been doing? I haven't seen any news —"

She stiffened and mashed her teeth together. "You *wouldn't* see any news, would you?" The runners controlled what went into the main pirate news feed, which conquests were featured, which people were captured. None of Razia's activities since the kidnapping fiasco had ever been posted.

"Simmer down, I meant from Harms. You captured Bodhi a few weeks ago? What have you been doing since?"

"Stupid Jarvis Loeb, but he's being a pain in the ass."

"So go after someone else."

"No." She gulped down her beer again. "I want Loeb."

"See, this is what gets you into trouble," Sage said with a shake of his head. "You get obsessed with something and then you don't stop until you get it."

"How is that a bad thing?"

"Because you often make stupid decisions to get there. Then, *I* have to bail you out."

"Like *one time*." She dramatically rolled her eyes. "And

I've never asked for your help."

"Uh-huh."

"Except that one time when I did, but that's because Lizbeth made me."

"And so you're telling me that you think if I hadn't saved your ass all those times, you would have been able to worm your way out yourself?"

"Uh, *yes*."

"Right." Sage sat back. "And so you're not going to give up on Loeb, even though he hasn't been caught in nearly ten years and it would take a damned miracle to capture him?"

She scowled; how did she not know that he hadn't been captured in ten years? It made sense, he was overly cautious and although he was high on the list, he didn't do much to separate himself from the pack. Most pirates tended to get captured once their ego got in the way of their common sense.

But damn it, she wanted to capture him. And if she did, perhaps she might get a little recognition.

"Your wheels are spinning," Sage said. "What are you thinking about? Are you even listening to me?"

"Mm."

"I swear, Lyss. You need to take a break once in a while."

"Yeah, I'll take a break when someone's put a bounty on my head," Razia grumbled. Her eyes landed at a table across the room and on Relleck, who noticed her at the same time. His eyes slid to Sage and he scowled.

If she were being honest, not wanting to spend time with Relleck was only partially about wanting to work. She wasn't quite sure she wanted to take that next official step with him. "I mean, who has time for dating anyway?"

"Dating, who said anything about dating?" A twinge of pink appeared on Sage's cheeks.

Razia cursed her buzz-induced slip-up and tried to salvage the situation. For some reason, she didn't think Sage would be too happy to find out that she was sneaking into dark alleys with Relleck. "It's…Lizbeth. She's got this idea that I work too much, and I need to have more fun."

"And that means dating?" Sage swallowed.

"From her standpoint, sure," Razia said, playing with the table. "You know, I'm not sure if there are any protocols, but I'm pretty sure I'm not allowed to date a guy in another web."

"What about if you dated someone in our web?" Sage asked, his voice an octave higher than normal.

"Like who? Eli Stenson? He's like...ninety." Razia laughed. The idea was ridiculous.

"I mean, there's other guys..."

"No." Razia glanced over at Relleck again, who downed another shot and looked like it tasted foul. "I don't even...I don't have time."

"I don't know, maybe Lizbeth is right," Sage shrugged. "You're still in the top twenty—"

"Because of my *stupid boss's blackmailing bounty*," she hissed, low enough so no one else would hear. "And that's… well…I'm pretty sure that's coming due soon." She chewed on her lip. "I need someone else to put a bounty on me or else I'm sunk."

"Do you want my…you know what, no." Sage shook his head. "I'm not even going to offer because you'll get pissy and bitchy about the mere offer of help."

"Good, you're learning." She looked at her mini-computer, as an alert just popped up. Loeb just made appearance at a poker game only two blocks from Eamon's. While she didn't think this would result in anything, she also would kick herself later if she didn't at least go monitor him.

She downed the rest of her beer. "Besides, I don't need your help anyway." She stood up in the booth seat and walked across the table, to the annoyance of the crew. She jumped down, taking a moment to steady herself. She'd had more than she thought.

"You okay to go after him?" Sage asked.

"'f course," she slurred, walking out the door.

***

Razia's eyes snapped open and she grasped at the wall to steady herself. She stood outside the supposed poker game location, in a dimly lit alley that smelled like trash. There was something wet leaking from the bin next to her, so she didn't dare sit down. She had fallen asleep against the dirty brick wall for a split second, but was now wide awake and ready for Loeb to come out.

The door remained closed.

Poker, she reasoned, must be Loeb's chosen vice because he'd been there playing this game for over an hour. She wondered how many times he'd have to go to Temple to ask the Great Creator for forgiveness for this break in his piety.

She snorted at her own joke then burped a little beer. She

rubbed her face roughly, hoping the increased blood flow would wake her up. She wished she hadn't had that that third beer (or however many she had from Sage's pitcher) at Eamon's, she wished she had some coffee, and she wished Loeb would just get a move on already. She had other pirates to capture, and he was being awfully selfish with her time.

She jutted her lip out and stared at the door, and her eyes began drooping again.

Her mini-computer began buzzing at her hip and she jumped ten feet. Scowling, she answered it without thinking.

"What." She blinked at the face looking back at her and for a brief moment saw Vel. With another shake of her head she realized it was Heelin scowling back at her. "Oh, it's you."

"Yes, it's me." Heelin looked nothing short of livid. "The brother with whom you are supposed to be working."

She grimaced. "Oh, God in Leveman's, I don't have time for this."

"Well you'd better *make* time, because this stupid planet was approved for membership, so Dorst wants me to accompany you on your next excavation."

Excavation, what was that again? She rubbed her eyes, trying to make sense of the word. Slowly, her brain readjusted from a month of bounty hunting back to her life as Lyssa Peate.

Wait…Heelin wanted to go on an excavation with her? "I don't think so."

"I think that you have to since Dorst ordered you to."

"I think that Dorst can get sucked."

"What is with you lately? You look different."

"I...what?" she said, looking down at the mini-computer.

"And where are you anyway? Are you in some kind of dark alley? Where are your glasses?"

Razia realized with a jolt of fear that she was, in fact, Razia and not Lyssa—her hair down, no lab coat, no glasses.

"Uh...gotta go!"

She ended the call quickly and breathed a sigh of relief. She didn't expect Heelin to recognize Razia from just a simple phone call. Unlike Lizbeth, who was sharp as a tack and made the connection almost immediately, the Peates seemed more eager to ignore that Lyssa ever existed.

Like Jukin.

She swallowed the lump in her throat, hating herself and her drunkenness for bringing him up. She still had no idea why she'd saved him. She'd told Lizbeth at the time it was because she wanted to believe he was a good person, but there was more to it than that. She was still harboring a little bit of guilt that *she* had been chosen as Sostas' assistant, and not Jukin.

And perhaps she felt a little responsible for everything Jukin had done.

She belched loudly in the alleyway, ending the drunken philosophical train of thought. In some part of her mind, she wondered if it was a good idea to be out in her current state, but then again, she was simply stalking Loeb. He wasn't going to surprise her and walk out...

Her eyes nearly fell out of her head as Jarvis Loeb exited the bar all by himself.

She braced herself against the wall, waiting to see if his

body men were going to join him. Loeb got almost a block before she realized that he was alone. Whether this was some great twist of fate, or maybe some gift from the Great Creator, she didn't know, but it was definitely an opportunity.

She nearly tripped over her own two feet as she barreled after him, the beer sloshing in her stomach uncomfortably.

"Oi!" she called out, standing in the middle of the deserted street.

Loeb turned to watch her with an amused look on his face. "Hello there, dear. Are you here to capture me finally?"

"Sure am!" she announced, perhaps louder than she should have.

She walked up to Loeb, who seemed awfully sober to her, and she reared back her fist to strike him. But she was moving so slow—slower than ever—and Loeb easily ducked it. She lurched forward, her center of gravity completely off, and watched the pavement fly up towards her face.

Loeb's hand clamped down on her wrist and she felt cold steel encircle it.

# CHAPTER THREE

Panic flooded her entire body as the second handcuff clinked into place.

"Wh-what are you doing?" she gasped, pulling her hands apart. She could only get an inch or two before the metal cut into her.

"I am catching a pirate who's been bothering me for a few weeks." Loeb laughed, his meaty hand landing on her shoulder. "Saw you'd spent a few hours at Eamon's. Pretty damned stupid for you to come after me after you'd been drinkin'."

"Y-you...wh...what?" Razia stammered, her mind too addled from beer and shock to process anything quickly.

He pushed her forward into the street, and she finally

realized what was happening.

"Hold on a second, *you can't capture me*!" she exclaimed.

"Oh, did I miss that news bulletin about girl pirates?" Loeb chuckled, his hand coming down on her shoulder again. "You play the game, you gotta lose sometimes."

Lose, she couldn't *lose*. Losing meant that her own bounty would be nulled out and back to zero.

She found herself uttering words she never thought she'd say. "How much can I pay you to let me go?"

"C'mon, darling, let's not do this," he tutted. "You wanted to run with the boys, didn't you?"

She whined. "It's not about that, it's…I'm different."

"So now you wanna be different?" Loeb chuckled. "You been saying all this time—"

She glared at him and shut her mouth. He wouldn't care how much shit Dissident was going to give her, or how her entire bounty was funded by one individual currently burning in Plethegon. Everything she had been working for, all of the hard work—it had vaporized right before her eyes.

She was *captured*.

She. Razia.

Captured.

She spotted the bright lights of Eamon's up ahead and turned to look at Loeb with a nervous expression on her face. "Do you have to walk me by Eamon's?"

"C'mon," he said, pushing her forward with a smile.

"Well…well…well…" Linro Lee was just leaving the bar and spotted her on the street. She glared at him; as if he had the right to sneer at her. She had captured him last year.

He walked up beside her and Loeb. Razia swallowed and kept her eyes on the ground, needing to keep focus on stoicism before she lost her temper. It would be even more embarrassing if she mouthed off in handcuffs.

"You get in those pants yet?" Linro said, reaching for Razia. Loeb knocked his hand away.

"Hands off my bounty." Razia thought she saw Loeb wink at her, but she put her eyes back on the ground. She became briefly aware that if someone like Lee had captured her instead of Loeb, she might be in a very different position. But that thought floated away as soon as more pirates fell out of the bar, hooting and laughing as they spotted her.

"Ooh, baby you look good in handcuffs."

"Yeah, I's saying, it was gonna be soon that someone was gonna get her."

"Looks like the little gnat got swatted!"

Something cold slipped into her stomach. Relleck stood in the front door at Eamon's, a heartless smirk on his face. There was no concern, there was no worry for her safety. Nothing but cold satisfaction at her predicament.

Oscillating between shock and hurt, she stared at him for a moment. He raised his eyebrows at her, as if daring her to say something to him. Instead, she closed her open mouth and forced herself to look forward, telling herself that Relleck was just trying to act natural. But somewhere deep inside, she knew he was being more honest with her than he'd ever been before.

"C'mon," Loeb said, pushing her forward.

***

The bounty office was blessedly empty that night, save for a few low-level pirates. The damage was done anyway; she was sure that news of her capture had spread like wildfire across Eamon's. But now, of course, the real pain was about to begin.

"Who's…aaah." The man at the bounty office window grinned, chewing on his cigarette as she glowered at him. It was the first time he had ever looked pleased to see her. "Seems about right."

"What's *that* supposed to mean?" Razia hissed.

The man simply chuckled and took Loeb's C-card, running it through the machine to transfer the bounty money to Loeb's account. Razia wondered for a brief moment if Loeb would be able to see who put the fifteen million bounty on her head, but that was a worry for another day. For now, she had other problems.

Two portly officers appeared at the door next to the bounty window. Loeb uncuffed her and nodded as the new hands clamped down on her shoulders and pulled her through the door.

Her eyes took a second to adjust to the bright lights on this side of the bounty office. She knew that she was now inside the ivory tower that loomed over the pirate city, albeit a long way from the pristine marble floors in the lobby. Grungy cubicles lined the room, inside of which officers typed away on computers and yukked it up with their supposed prisoners. When she and her officer passed, their conversations ceased, then picked up with more ardent fervor.

None of the officers had the gold-trimmed markings of

Jukin's idiots, which made sense, of course. Everything in this room was funded by the runners. The entire system of piracy was predicated on this one activity—when a pirate was captured, they suffered nothing but humiliation and the loss of their bounty. One night in jail, and the pirate was free to go.

Razia plopped down in an empty cubicle and was joined by a man with pockmarked skin, stubble, and a disheveled uniform.

"So…Razia," the officer, named Dipzenski, drawled. "Heard of you."

Her hopes lifted slightly. "Really?"

"Yeah, I'd heard there was a girl running around these parts. Only a matter of time before you get caught, huh?"

Instead of responding, she focused her eyes on the piece of paper held to his cubicle wall by a pushpin. On it were a list of office codes for the Universal Police. She tried very hard to memorize them, if only to ignore where she currently sat.

"Says here you kidnapped—oh, that's right," he laughed as he sat back in his squeaky chair, "you kidnapped ol' Joke Peate's brother."

Razia tore her eyes from the codes as she processed what he'd said. "*Joke* Peate?"

"Yeah," Dipzenski laughed, rubbing his belly. "We all just think he's so full of himself. He prances around here once a week, checking our paperwork." He snorted. "Idiot."

"Yep." Razia was in no mood to have a conversation about Jukin. Or conversation period.

"So, you ever done this before?" he asked, typing into his

computer again. He squinted at his screen then his eyes widened. "No! We got ourselves a virgin here!"

Razia groaned and sank down lower as the word echoed across the police station. A few of the officers turned to look at her, smirking and laughing.

"Can you stop, please?" she whispered.

"No, no, a first timer is a big deal," Dipzenski said, sitting back. "Who got you, huh?"

She clenched her jaw. "Loeb."

"Ah, ol' Jarvy, huh? Yeah, he's not been in here for a long time, but we see his handiwork! So how'd he do it?"

"I don't want to talk about it."

But Dipzenski wasn't about to let her go that easily. "C'mon, that's half the fun! You tell me, I tell my buddy, and that's—"

"How Harms gets his information," Razia grumbled. She closed her eyes and forced out, "*I made a mistake.*"

"Yeah, how so?"

"That's all you're getting," Razia hissed at him. "If you want more, talk to Loeb when I capture him once I get outta here."

"That's all, you say..." He grunted and looked at the computer. "And I say maybe I'll give Captain Peate a call and see if he's interested in bringing you in. Maybe he wants to talk to you about kidnapping his brother."

Razia's eyes narrowed. "You can't do that. I'm in the web."

"Eh, one or two slips through the cracks, nobody'd notice."

She sputtered angrily, but she knew these cops weren't above corrupt behavior. And Dissident wouldn't throw a stink if she ended up in a *real* jail instead of the pirate one. Or worse, the compound on the other side of D-882 where Tauron was put to death.

She recounted the events of her capture as she remembered them., pushing the words out through clenched teeth. Dipzenski watched with a sadistic smile as she spoke, and she felt disgusting. Her story seemed to sate his voyeuristic desire, and he continued booking her.

"Since this is your first time, we gotta put you through the process, huh?" he said, typing more. "Finger prints, mug shots—"

"I have a mug shot," she insisted. Tauron took it for her, and she was rather fond of it. She looked angry and powerful.

But Dipzenski wasn't listening to her and pulled out a camera, snapping a photo before she even knew what was happening. The photo that came up on his computer was similarly perplexed.

Razia blanched. "That's terrible."

"Eh, nobody'll see it. That's just for us." His lewd smile made Razia wonder where in Leveman's they got these officers. Then again, he was completely obstructing the law by letting her run free in a few hours, so his moral compass was already skewed.

Dipzenski took his sweet time finishing her booking, stopping for fifteen minutes to chat with a buddy across the hall about the latest sports game while she fumed in anger. She just wanted this entire miserable episode to be over.

But as was the pattern for the day, her misery was prolonged. After the booking came the fingerprint-taking with another officer, who also wanted to know the particulars of how she was captured. He also took the liberty of commenting about how females couldn't hold their liquor, and Razia's tongue was nearly bleeding from biting it. Once they had her fingerprints, then Dipzenski led her to the prison itself, which sat at the basement of the U-POL ivory tower. The room was dark and musty, with a small trickle of light streaming in through a dirty window. One half-burnt out light illuminated a pasty, overweight officer watching a television.

"Oi!" Dipzenski barked at the other officer, causing the latter to pull his feet off of the table slowly. He rose to his feet and began typing on the old computer at his desk.

"So," Razia turned around and Dipzenski was gone. She rolled her eyes at the pure lack of professionalism displayed by every single one of these officers. Turning back to the portly officer standing by the computer, she folded her arms over her chest to wait for whatever hoops he wanted her to jump through.

"Empty your pockets," he grunted, thrusting a dented metal box at her.

She unhooked her belt and slammed it into the box, glaring at him as she did so. "There."

"And the mini, too."

She started, her fingers tightening around her trusty mini-computer. The thought of being parted with it sent an irrational jolt of fear down her spine.

"Can't I keep it?"

"Them's the rules," the officer said, jiggling the box. "Put it in."

"But you guys don't pay attention to the rules—"

"Put it in."

"But!" Before she could say another word, he reached over with a swiftness that was alarming for a man his size and snatched her precious mini-computer, placing it in the bin and yanking it out of her reach. She suddenly felt cold and anxious, needing to check all manner of statistics. But, as the officer turned the key on the wall of lockers, she knew she wasn't going to see it again for at least a night.

He took his time waddling out of the small desk area, leading her down a long stretch of iron doors with windows too tall for her to see inside. She wondered who'd been captured tonight, who had been stupid like her. If Eamon's was any indication, it was probably nobody interesting, since everybody who was anybody had witnessed the mortifying episode.

A fresh wave of embarrassed shame fell over her as the memory replayed.

The officer stopped in front of a door just like all the rest and slid his keycard on the swiper. The door groaned as it opened, revealing a stark white room with a single cot in the corner.

"In ya go." His sweaty hand on her shoulder shoved her inside, and before she could bark at him, the door slammed shut.

Then silence.

So much silence.

She cleared her throat, the sound bouncing off the blank white walls. She spun around and looked at the white steel door with a high window that she couldn't see out of. There was a wool blanket on the cot, but nothing else in the room.

She shuffled over to the corner and sat down on the bed. It squeaked loudly.

She was suddenly aware of her own breathing, the quiet hum of the air coming through the vent, the buzzing of the light overhead. An overwhelming urge to check her mini-computer surfaced, and she breathed deeply to quiet it. She wouldn't be in there but a few hours. It was simply a formality that she sit there for some amount of time to allow the consequence-free game of piracy to continue unabated.

She really could have been in a worse situation, she tried to tell herself. If she hadn't been in the web, if she'd been captured by one of Jukin's Special Forces...or, she winced, if she'd been captured by someone like Linro Lee, who might not have brought her to the bounty office at all.

The thought made her shudder and feel even dumber for putting herself in such a dangerous position. Getting into a fight drunk was probably the stupidest thing she'd ever done, and she had done some stupid things.

That's probably why Sage hovered over her.

Except, she realized with a jolt, he hadn't been really hovering lately and he hadn't for some time. He had let her walk out of Eamon's with naught but a casual query of her inebriation. Perhaps he'd finally decided he was done coddling her and would let her stand on her own two feet.

And now she was sitting in a jail cell.

He was going to be as bad as Dissident probably, with a big, hearty, "I told you so." She could already see his smug face.

He was right. About everything.

Balling up her fist, she slammed it into the mattress in anger, and winced as the odd angle shot pain up her arm. Now she'd hurt herself. And she was stuck in jail. And her bounty had been zeroed out.

She heard the squeak of the bed and realized she was tapping her foot distractedly on the floor. With a heaving and not-at-all-satisfying sigh, she leaned against the wall and looked up at the white ceiling.

If it was difficult to get noticed in the top twenty, it was going to be downright impossible to do now that she wasn't even *on* the list. She could capture every pirate in the known universe, but her bounty wouldn't move an inch unless someone else thought she was worth catching.

With a heavy sigh, she wrapped the scratchy blanket tight around herself and curled into a small ball on the mattress, hoping to drown out that voice with sleep.

***

A noise startled her awake; her cell door was being unlocked. With no clocks in the room, she had no idea what time it was, but perhaps her one night stint in jail was complete.

What she didn't expect to see was Sage pop his head in the doorway, a smug grin on his face.

"What are you doing here?" she asked, wondering if she

was still half-asleep.

"Heard you got captured, wanted to see it for myself." He leaned against the doorframe. "Well, I would say I told you so but that would be..." He paused and chuckled. "Oh, why not. Told you so."

"Get sucked," she hissed. His face was just as she imagined it the night before. "Are you just here to gloat?"

"A little, yeah." His grin widened when she snarled at him. "Nah, I'm here to get you, since your ship has been so conveniently parked back at that scientist place."

"My ship..." She'd completely forgotten about it, parked at an expensive docking station far on the outskirts of the city. But then again, she'd only been away from it for a day. "Why did you take my ship?"

"Because I'm kidnapping you," he said before adding, "Wouldn't be the first time."

She rubbed her face, too tired for that memory to elicit a painful response. "Wh...what do you mean?"

"Look, you've been running yourself ragged for the past few weeks," Sage said. "You're exhausted—look at you."

"Am not."

"We—me, Lizbeth, and Vel from whatever planet he's currently surviving on, we all think you need to take a break."

She stared at him for a second, only the first part of his statement making sense. "How in Leveman's did you get in touch with Vel?"

"Okay, so I didn't speak to him, but I'm sure he'd agree," Sage said with a grin. "C'mon." He stepped into the cell and offered his hand to help her out of the bed. "What are friends for, hm?"

"I'm not your *friend*," she snapped, slapping his hand away and marching out of the jail.

Sage followed her down the hall, stopping to wave at some of the other pirates in the cells. Razia was thankful she was too short to be seen through the windows on the doors.

She came to the end of the cellblock where a different U-POL officer than the night before sat watching a television. She stood in front of the counter for a few breaths, waiting for the officer to notice her standing there. But he was engrossed, or didn't care.

"I need my stuff," Razia said to get his attention.

He grunted at her, ran a hand lazily across his rotund belly, and made no move to go to the set of lockers behind him.

"Come *on*." Razia just wanted to get out of there already.

"Eh?" He turned his head slightly to look at her then slowly, painfully, and deliberately turned around in his chair and waddled over to the lockers.

"Which one are you?"

Razia resisted the urge to roll her eyes. "Razia. You know, the only woman that you've seen in here in…ever?"

He grunted again and opened a locker, pulling out a small box. He placed the box on the desk and checked his tablet.

"One utility belt."

Razia snatched it as soon as she could reach it, rehooking it around her waist.

"One set of handcuffs."

Again, Razia took her things, but her eye was on the

mini-computer at the bottom of the box. She hadn't gone this long without looking at it, and she was getting twitchy.

"And one mini-computer—"

"I'll take that." Sage appeared at her shoulder and took the instrument before she could get her fingers on it.

"Hey!" Razia spun around, livid.

Sage held it above his head, just out of her reach."No, you need to detox. No mini-computer for you."

"*Give it back!*" Razia jumped up and down, but as Sage towered above her by almost a foot, she was unable to grab it. She latched onto his arm and swung from it, swiping and grasping at the air, and he shoved her off.

"Oy!" the U-POL officer snarled from behind the glass. "Take the rest of yer stuff too."

Razia, still furious, snatched her floating canvas and disks from the table and stuffed them into her utility belt. By the time she spun back around to yell at Sage, he was halfway out the door.

"*Get back here!*" she screamed, running after him. She burst out of the back room into the main bounty holding area, and immediately felt the eyes of everyone in the room. But she no longer cared that they knew she'd been captured; she had a blond pirate to murder.

She saw Sage talking with Jeam Bullock, who was bringing Max Fried to the bounty office and she marched over.

"*Give me back my mini-computer you son of a bitch,*" she growled through gritted teeth.

"Oh, it's you," Bullock said, looking like someone had

just handed him something foul. "Nice work getting captured, moron."

"Get sucked, you were captured last week," Razia said, waving him off before turning to Sage and lunging for her mini-computer. "*Give it back!*"

"No."

She balled her hands into fists and groaned loudly.

"Calm down." Sage tossed her mini-computer into the waiting hands of Ganon, who pocketed it. Razia was so furious that she hadn't even seen him standing there. "Let's go."

"Go?" She blinked at him. "Go where?"

"Vacation, remember?" he said, wrapping his arm around her shoulder. She struggled against the unfamiliar feeling, but he had a firm grip on her. "See ya, Bullock."

Bullock grunted and Razia heard him mutter something about the two of them that made her want to get as far away from Sage as possible.

Unfortunately, Sage's iron grip didn't let up until they were safely on his ship.

# CHAPTER FOUR

Sage's ship was moderately sized, as far as pirate ships went. There were three levels, the lowest for storage and on-boarding, the second level comprised of five bedrooms, and the upper level for a small conference area and the bridge, where Sage and Ganon disappeared to after they arrived. Which was a good thing, because if Lyssa had to look at them for another second, she might tear off one of Sage's appendages.

Huffing and puffing, she remained on the lower level with Sage's equipment until she could at least see straight. She wanted her mini-computer; she didn't want to be *kidnapped.* She needed to get back to work. But Sage didn't listen to her cries of protest, and so she watched out of the window as

D-882 disappeared.

"Vacation," she scoffed, running her hands along the netting holding the space jump gear against the wall. She and Lizbeth had gone to Sage for help breaking into the Universal Bank, and they'd used this very same gear to descend onto the planet. She briefly considered using the gear to escape Sage's ship, but considering how he jumped after her—not to mention her fear of falling—she decided against it.

Resigning herself to this fate, at least for now, she began the slow climb up the stairs. She paused on the second level and slowly walked down the short hallway. She counted five doors, two on either side and one on the end, which she made a beeline for.

Immediately, she knew it was Sage's bedroom, if not from the location and the size, but from the way it smelled. It wasn't a bad odor, but something about it was comforting and familiar. She opened the door wider and turned on the light, illuminating the posters of naked women on the metal walls above the bed.

Men will be men, she supposed. Tauron had the same set up in his room, too.

Sage's bed was sizable, bigger than her one-person mattress, and he had a collection of blankets and a maroon comforter balled on top as if he'd thrown them off and walked out the door. That was, at least, how he used to get up. In the corner, she spotted an open closet with a two-foot high pile of wrinkled shirts and pants. She left the closet alone, if memory served what he kept under his dirty clothes.

Without another thought, she walked over to the unmade

bed and flopped down on it, catching even more of that familiar scent. It made her smile and daydream about weekends and semester breaks arguing over whose socks were smelling and whose trash was on whose side, and all manner of other things that Lyssa forgot about as she drifted off to sleep.

When she awoke some hours later, she felt refreshed and in a much better mood. She hadn't gotten sleep like that in a while. She stretched and realized she was curled up underneath Sage's cheap, scratchy comforter and blankets and her boots and socks had been pulled off. She lazed around for a minute, running her bare feet along the rough cotton sheets, a sleepy smile on her face.

She tilted her head down to gaze around the room and noticed a black duffle bag on the floor that wasn't there before. Curious, she got up and padded over to the bag, kneeling down and unzipping it. Her own clothes were stuffed inside—shirts, shorts, even a few sets of bras and underwear. The idea of Sage in her closet made her both queasy and amused, but she was actually rather thankful. She'd been in these same clothes since before she was captured and she needed a shower.

Sage's bathroom was attached to his room. The only towel she could locate was threadbare, and some very old looking rags would have to suffice as washcloths. She showered quickly, as she remembered what showering on an all-male pirate ship was like. She stepped out of the shower and toweled herself off, quickly putting on her bra and underwear (usually the first things to disappear) and wrapping the towel around her hair. She stepped out of the bathroom and nearly jumped out of her skin.

"Oh shit, sorry," Sage said, nearly falling off his bed.

"You *scared* me," Lyssa said, her hand covering her heart. She was surprisingly fine with him seeing her like this; after all, they shared a room when they were kids. Although he seemed to be blushing something fierce.

"Thanks for the clothes," she said, plucking a shirt out of the duffle bag and sliding it over her wet hair.

Sage coughed, his face even brighter. "No worries, Lizbeth said—"

"Lizbeth?" Lyssa's head swiveled around as she pulled on a pair of cargo pants. "Is she going to be wherever we're going? And how long am I going to be there for that matter? And where am I going?"

"In order: Yes, a week, and I'm not telling."

Lyssa muttered something about him being a jackass, but then furrowed her brow in thought. Since the assassination attempt, she really hadn't seen Lizbeth in person but once or twice. Lizbeth had been promoted twice to lead investigator and was trying to tie up the loose ends of the conspiracy. If Lyssa had to be kidnapped and held hostage, at least she'd have some good company.

"What?" Sage asked, watching her face contort as her mind worked.

"Just thinking this won't be so bad if Lizbeth's going to be there." Lyssa crouched on her haunches and dug through her bag, hunting for some clean socks.

"You two seemed to have really hit it off," Sage said, an

odd expression on his face. "Are you…seeing her?"

Lyssa nearly fell off her heels and she blanched at Sage. "What?"

"Other than Vel, she seems to be the only thing you show any affection for." Another blush rose to Sage's face. "I mean, it's okay if—"

"I'm not dating *her*," Lyssa said, with enough emphasis on "her" to pique Sage's curiosity.

"Then who are you dating?"

"Nobody," she snapped. Relleck's face at the bounty office floated back into her mind. She shook her head to clear the image; that was obviously over. "You know me. I don't do that crap."

"Yeah, I know." Sage shrugged and offered a sly smile. "Still, it's nice to see you branching out."

Instead of responding to his comment, she asked, "Did you pack me twenty pairs of underwear and zero socks?"

"I wouldn't worry about it, you won't be wearing clothes much anyway." The moment the words left his mouth, he seemed to immediately regret them. His face turned the brightest red she'd ever seen and he stood up stammering idiotically. "I mean, never mind. I just came by to tell you that…uh…if you're hungry…there's food…and we'll be there…in a bit."

Lyssa wasn't able to respond before he bolted out the door.

She sat in the quiet room, wondering what in Leveman's had just transpired, but desperately needing a pair of socks to warm her increasingly chilly feet. When she found none in the bag (*damn Teon*), she slid on the socks she had been wearing and laced up her boots, as those were the only shoes she had, too.

She climbed the last set of stairs to the top level of the ship and made her way to the bridge. Like the ship itself, it was modest in size, with room for the pilot and mechanic, and, of course, Sage's captain's chair in the center of the room. She noticed he had installed (poorly, she might add) some monitors which were currently set to the pirate intraweb. Small pictures of pirates flipped over each other on the most wanted list and her fingers itched to start hunting.

Before she got two steps in, the screens went blank.

"Good morning, princess!" Ganon was standing behind the screens with the plug hanging from his hands. "So lovely of you to join us."

"Where's Sage?" she asked, looking around the bridge. The only other person was Sobal, the young computer hacker. "Actually, where is…everyone?"

"Boss gave them the week off," Ganon said, resuming his place at the helm of the ship.

"So why are you still here?"

"Because I thought it would be highly entertaining to watch you twist in the breeze." Ganon snorted. "Fighting drunk. what is this, amateur hour?"

Lyssa was about to snap at him, but stopped herself. She really had no right to argue with him. So instead, she flopped down on Sage's captain's seat and kicked her heels up on the table as she'd seen Sage do countless times.

"You can't sit there," Sobal said, sounding very much like

the petulant young man that he was. "That's the boss' chair. Anybody who sits there gets dish duty for a week."

"I'd like to see him try," Lyssa scoffed, leaning back. She looked up at the screen in front of her, spotting the navigational application in the bottom corner, and the destination. "C-47478462?"

"Yep," Ganon said and added under his breath, "Middle of frickin' nowhere."

Lyssa chewed on her thumb. Why did that planet sound familiar? She'd never excavated any C-planets before, but something about…

"Lizbeth's parents?" she said suddenly.

"We have a winner!" Ganon said, tossing a look back at her.

"Parents…" Lyssa leaned back into the chair and suddenly growing nervous. From the way Lizbeth had described her parents, they seemed harmless enough, but memories of going "home" to the Manor still stung. She suddenly craved a distraction. "Hey, can I get my mini-computer back now?"

Ganon groaned loudly and Sobal whooped loudly. Lyssa heard footsteps behind them and turned to see Sage appear on the bridge, finally.

"Oh shit…did she?" he asked, as if he'd run up the set of stairs.

"Yes," Ganon snarled, pulling out his mini-computer and Sage did the same. Lyssa looked between the two of them, blinking madly.

"W…what's going on?"

"We had a bet," Sobal grinned, kicking his feet up on the table in front of him as Lyssa had done (one stern look from Sage and they were back down). "How long until you'd ask for your mini back. Sage thought you'd last the day, Ganon said you'd last until we reached the planet, at least!"

"Thought you'd be asleep for longer," Ganon grumbled.

"But I said that within ten minutes of showing up on the bridge, you'd be asking for it!" Sobal announced proudly. "So I win a hundred credits each!"

***

Except for a few open fields, D-66253 was completely covered in tall, thick pine-looking trees and it was in one of those fields that Ganon landed Sage's giant pirate ship. Lyssa walked down the dock and looked around. For a second, she forgot that she was on a residential planet and thought she was on some planet excavation. The fresh air gave her the urge to run, but she didn't see her running shoes in her duffel bag.

She rolled her eyes. No socks and no running shoes. Sage might as well have packed her a garbage bag.

In the distance, a small dust-up looked to be coming their way. When it drew closer, Lyssa saw that it was actually a small four-wheeled truck. Most planets had transport shuttles, but cars were prevalent on some of the residential ones to get from place to place without the need for a larger ship.

When the truck stopped, a mop of curly light brown hair emerged from the passenger's side and came running over.

"LYSS!" Lizbeth wore a giant grin and a simple white t-shirt with short cut-off jeans. Before Lyssa could even react, Lizbeth threw herself at her, enveloping her in a hug.

"Hey there," Ganon grinned, but Lizbeth wasn't paying attention to him.

"Oh, I am so happy you're here!" Lizbeth said, cupping Lyssa's face. She frowned and stared at the space between Lyssa's eyebrows. "You haven't been plucking."

Lyssa brushed her off. "I've been busy."

"No matter, I've got a pair of tweezers in my bag." Lizbeth looped her arm through Lyssa's. "Come meet my dad!"

The word "dad" sent chills down Lyssa's spine, but she couldn't say no to the boisterous government investigator. So she allowed herself to be dragged over to the truck, where a tall man with a pleasant smile was waiting. Lyssa could see a little bit of Lizbeth in him, especially when he pulled her into a big hug.

"So this is the gal who helped Lizzie save the government!" He smiled down at her proudly, as if Lyssa were his own daughter. The sentiment was weird to Lyssa, but she tried not to dwell on it.

"Yeah." Lyssa forced herself to smile back.

"Call him Joe," Lizbeth said, ignorant of Lyssa's discomfort. "Or Dad, either way."

Lyssa hadn't called anyone "dad" in…ever, and she wasn't about to start now.

"Joe," she said with a smile and a nervous nod.

"And Dad, this is Sage and two of his friends," Lizbeth said, motioning to the other three, who had clamored off the ship as well. Lyssa saw Sage had her duffle bag and another one slung over his shoulder. He reached out his free hand to shake Joe's hand with a firm grip that made his blood vessels pop in his forearm.

"Ganon and Sobal," Sage said, motioning behind to the other two, the former closing up the ship and locking it. Sobal was ladened with both his and Ganon's bag.

"Great to have you!" Joe beamed at all of them. "Now hop in the truck. The girls can ride in the cab and boys and bags in the back!"

Lyssa, still absorbing the situation, wordlessly climbed in next to Lizbeth while Sage tossed all the bags in the back and then hopped in.

"You boys hang on!" Joe called, adjusting his rearview mirror. "Girls, buckle up, okay? Your momma would kill me if anything happened to you."

Lizbeth laughed and kissed her father on the cheek and Lyssa suddenly felt the cab was too small.

With a roar, the engine turned over and the truck spun around, Joe putting on a little more speed than necessary to have a bit of fun with all the occupants. Laughter filtered in from the open window and she turned her head to look at the three guys clinging to the edge of the truck. She caught Sage's eye, and he winked at her.

Quickly, she turned back around to face the front.

"So, Lyss," Joe said, and Lyssa wondered when she gave him permission to call her that, "Lizzie tells me that you're one of the best bounty hunters in the universe."

Lyssa suddenly remembered why she was there and slumped.

"Oh, baby," Lizbeth said, wrapping her arm around

Lyssa, "it's going to be okay. You just had a bad day. Happens to all of us."

"Yeah."

"Look, we're going to have a fun week!" Lizbeth squeezed Lyssa again. "Daddy's going to take us tubing, and we can spend some time out on the boat, just the seven of us. You, me, Momma, Daddy, Sage, Ganon, and Sobal."

Lyssa wanted her running shoes more than anything now.

"She'll buck up," Lizbeth said to her father. "She's just in shock. And she's a bit of a sourpuss."

Lyssa glared at her friend but was soon distracted by the house that seemed to appear in the middle of the thick forest. In fact, it looked constructed out of the very same wood that grew in the trees. Which made sense, Lyssa's DSE brain reasoned. D-planets were residential because they could be self-sufficient and didn't require a lot of shipping in or out.

The truck rumbled to a stop in the driveway, and Lyssa heard all of the guys hop out the truck bed, remarking on the house and the lot.

"And the lake's behind the house," Joe commented, slamming the door shut behind him.

"Are we gonna get out?" Lizbeth asked Lyssa, who was still transfixed by the house.

"Y-yeah." Lyssa opened the truck door and stepped onto the gravel driveway, letting Lizbeth crawl out after her. Lyssa surveyed her surroundings, from the three-level house with the wrap-around balconies, to the way the trees towered over them. Everything looked warm and inviting, and it made her highly uncomfortable.

"Is that her?"

Lyssa's attention was drawn to a middle-aged woman on the second tier of the house. She wore an apron that was covered in flour, and a very familiar smile on her face as she descended the staircase two-by-two. She didn't even ask before pulling Lyssa into yet another hug.

"My goodness, look at you." Lizbeth's mother grinned at her. "Oh, I'm sorry, darling, I got you covered in flour. Well, not to worry about that. We'll get you into some more comfortable clothes. I'm sure you're burning up in those long sleeves. Do you want anything? Some wine, perhaps? I just opened a new bottle and—"

"Mom!" Lizbeth cut her off. "Give her a second to breathe, will ya? Lyssa, this is my mom, Billie."

"Nice to meet you," Lyssa managed to choke out.

"Let's let everyone get settled before you bombard them again," Lizbeth said, taking Lyssa's arm and guiding her up the staircase. "We don't have enough rooms for everyone, so you and I get to bunk together, and the guys are sharing a room, too."

Lyssa barely heard anything else that Lizbeth said, still overwhelmed by everything. In less than a day, she had gone from hunting a pirate on D-882, to being captured by that pirate, to being kidnapped by Sage, and now was at Lizbeth's parents' house on a forced vacation. Her head began to hurt, especially as Billie hovered behind them, talking about all the things that they might need or do need for dinner. The house was rustic but refined, and a brand new kitchen covered in half-completed baked goods welcomed them, as well as a grand view to a vast, sparkling lake.

"Wow!" Sage brushed past them, placing his and Lyssa's bags on the ground and taking in the sight of the lake. He and Joe than engaged in a conversation about the lake, the boat, and something else that was drowned out by the sound of Billie asking Lyssa if she wanted anything to eat or drink, and then the sound of Lizbeth asking her if she wanted to go explore the lake, and Sobal and Ganon arguing about something and—

"*I need a minute*!"

Lyssa rushed out of the house and down to the truck where she was finally able to take a deep breath. The silence of the forest calmed her down enough that she began feel a little silly for her reaction.

She looked at the truck under her fingertips and her mind drifted to the man who drove it. Joe was nothing like Sostas, and Billie was nothing like Eleonora, but something about Lizbeth's parents made Lyssa nervous. Still, it was pretty clear to see where Lizbeth got her moxie, her gumption, and her insufferable need to care about Lyssa.

Speaking of…

"You okay there, champ?" Lizbeth asked from the balcony.

"Yep."

"Please try not to be a total bitch the whole time you're here, huh?"

Lyssa spun around to glare daggers at Lizbeth, but realized the other woman was taunting her with a playful smile on her face.

"It's…a lot," Lyssa said, motioning to the house. "I'm not used to it."

"What, people?" Lizbeth chuckled, walking down the stairs to join her. "I know my mom is a bit much, but she's just excited. She'll calm down soon."

"Can I have my mini-computer back now?"

"Nope, you are on detox." Lizbeth wrapped her arm around Lyssa and pulling her back to the house. "Now, about that glass of wine…"

***

Dinner was a loud and boisterous affair, and it reminded Lyssa painfully of dinners at the Manor when she was growing up. At the Carter house, though, diners were not seated in age-order and no one was glaring daggers at her. Joe was a master storyteller, spinning tales about his time working for the UBU.

Lyssa couldn't help but notice that Lizbeth's parents seemed to beam every time Lizbeth interrupted with a correction about how things were *now* at the UBU versus how they used to be when Joe and Billie worked there. Interrupting Sostas like that would have resulted in a five minute tirade about how useless Lyssa was. And her own mother would have cut her arm off before admitting that she was proud of Lyssa for anything.

The conversation turned to piracy, and Sage and Ganon spent the better part of an hour retelling their best and most outrageous jobs, including one about a fake diamonds that sent them on a space jump.

"I swear, I didn't think the kid was gonna get through

that system," Ganon said, a proud smile to Sobal who blushed in his dinner. "Had to give him some tough love."

"I thought I was gonna hurl during that space jump," Sobal added meekly.

"Remember our space jump?" Lizbeth said to Lyssa.

"Lizbeth Adelyn!" Billie cried. "You jumped out of a spaceship?"

"Calm down, Mom," Lizbeth said, waving her off. "I jumped with Ganon! I'm not an idiot like *some people.*" She nodded towards Lyssa, who returned her look with a glare and a small blush.

"I can tell there's a story here," Joe said.

"Well," Sage said, sitting back, "Lyssa is afraid of heights —"

"*I am not afraid of heights,*" Lyssa snapped. To the three dubious expressions pointed her way, she added, "I just don't like to fall."

"Whatever," Sage said. "Anyway, Lyssa decided she was going to jump by herself, even though she had no idea where the drop site was and hadn't actually jumped in a good five years."

"So guess who had to jump out and rescue her!" Lizbeth added.

Lyssa's blush deepened. "He didn't *rescue* me!"

"How romantic!" Billie cooed, stars in her eyes.

Lyssa raised her eyebrow in confusion. Beside her, Lizbeth shook her head to quiet her mother.

"So then, Lizzie tells me you two go way back," Joe said to Lyssa and Sage. "How'd you meet?"

"Tauron made the unfortunate mistake of trying to kidnap her," Sage said, with a smile that told Lyssa he wasn't going into specifics, and for that she was grateful. "And then we couldn't get rid of her."

The table roared with laughter. Lyssa didn't mind that version of the story, so she smiled along with him.

"How old were you?" Lizbeth asked.

"Eleven." Sage answered for Lyssa.

"My goodness," Billie tutted.

"Well, I mean…" Sage chuckled. "It's not like Tauron wanted her to stay or anything. But she's kind of a force of nature."

"If *that* isn't the understatement of the century," Lizbeth chimed in with a playful wink.

"What do you mean he never wanted me to stay?" Lyssa asked.

"C'mon, Lyss. Like he wanted Jukin's sister hanging around his pirate ship," Sage said. "Leveman's, it took him a few years to even get used to the idea of letting a *girl* on his ship."

"Years?" Lyssa blinked in confusion.

"I think he thought you'd grow out of it," Sage continued. "But you're nothing if not stubborn."

Something cold slipped into her stomach. Sage spoke about Tauron as if he'd never wanted her around. That wasn't how she remembered it.

"Actually, I never could figure out," Sobal said, his mouth stuffed with food. "So Jukin, right? If he captured and killed Tauron's whole crew…then how'd *you* get away, Sage?"

Lyssa's attention suddenly shifted to Sage as a shadow fell across his face. In fact, the entire table seemed to notice the shift in the mood, except for Sobal, who continued shoveling food into his mouth.

When Sage opened his mouth to speak, it was very calm and very unlike him. "After Jukin and his squad of officers cornered Tauron's ship at a transport station, we knew we weren't making it out, and we also knew that Jukin had been threatening..." He trailed off, his voice strained. "So before Jukin boarded the ship, Tauron beat me to a bloody pulp and told Jukin I was a prisoner they were holding for ransom. And...so..." He paused, again considering his words. "Jukin let me go."

"Wow, that was brilliant of him—" Sobal seemed to finally notice the tension in the room and had the courtesy to shut up.

Lyssa knew the rest of the story that no one cared to ask about. Jukin had executed Tauron and the crew in a widely publicized spectacle. She'd witnessed it on a grainy monitor at the Academy. Her relief at seeing Sage at Harms' was immeasurable.

But the pain etched on Sage's face said enough.

"Excuse me for a second," Sage murmured, standing up and disappearing out the back door.

"Well, who wants dessert?" Billie offered, her cheeriness falling flat in the silent room.

Lyssa, however, was incensed.

"You are a goddamned *moron*," she growled at Sobal as she stood up. With a hard *thwap* to the back of the teenager's head, she followed Sage out onto the back deck.

He leaned against the railing and stared into the dark night with an unreadable expression. He didn't acknowledge her presence, but he also didn't startle when she sidled up beside him.

"You okay?" she asked.

He let out a long sigh instead of responding, and Lyssa felt the urge to comfort him in some way, although she didn't really know how.

"Just don't like to be reminded of that, you know," he whispered after a moment. "I wish…" He trailed off, and a fake smile plastered on his face. "Never mind. Did I hear something about dessert?"

"Stop it. You're pissed off at Jukin and—"

"I'm not pissed at Jukin," Sage whispered. "I'm pissed at Tauron."

Lyssa couldn't believe her ears. "Tauron? Why?"

"Because I should have died on that ship with the rest of the crew."

He spoke softly and with such certitude that Lyssa almost found herself nodding until she processed the meaning of his words. Her face shifted into a scowl.

"What are you talking about?" she hissed at him. "Died? Why do you think Tauron saved your life?"

"Honestly?" Sage asked, throwing his hands in the air. "I don't…I don't know."

Lyssa couldn't understand how he could be so stupid. "Because you were the kid," she said, and the reference caused her to smile even though she was ranting. Sage, predictably, bristled at the name, but not as much as when he was eighteen. "You were the kid and I was the brat, and...Tauron wouldn't have let anything happen to us. None of the crew would have."

"I guess I thought that since I was on the crew, I should have..." He trailed off. "I feel guilty that I'm here and they're...not."

Lyssa paused and thought for a moment. "But I think it's like...when you really care about someone, sure, you give them a lot of shit, but you'd still do anything to protect them."

Amused, Sage turned to look at her.

"What?"

"You." He laughed. "Talking about real people feelings. Lizbeth's been a good influence on you."

"You know what?" She smacked him playfully on the shoulder. "Jackass."

"That must mean you really care for me, Lyss."

She bristled, huffing and looking forward. She couldn't keep the smile off of her face, though.

"Do you?"

"What?"

"Care about me?"

She turned to look at him like he had two heads. "What kind of a dumbass question is that, Sage?"

He turned to look at her, and she saw something new in his eyes. She couldn't place her finger on it, but it made her squeamish, like she was seeing the inside of a human body.

"Do you care about me?" he repeated, a little quieter.

"Of course I do," she whispered, looking forward. Her heart raced and her palms were wet, but for the life of her, she couldn't figure out why. It was just Sage.

"You know, I had a plan," Sage said, changing the subject abruptly, "to get them out."

"Oh yeah?" Lyssa asked, grateful for the shift in topic. "You and what army?"

"Don't need an army. That entire prison was built poorly, you know. So easy to re-route alarm signals."

"The problem is, of course, getting to the prison," Lyssa said. "You know, since it's on the other side of D-882 from the city and surrounded by miles and miles of scorching desert."

He paused and cleared his throat. "Well, once I got into the prison, my plan would have worked."

"Yeah okay." She laughed. "Anyway, you're okay, right?"

"Yeah." He smiled and her heart began fluttering again as he wrapped his arm around her shoulder and pulled her in tight. They so rarely touched, but she found she didn't mind the way she fit under his chin like a glove. She breathed him in deep, remembering how comfortable it was in his room, sleeping in his bed. "Thanks for checking on me."

"Oh, Leveman's, don't get mushy," she snapped, pushing him away and walking back inside to regain control over herself.

# CHAPTER FIVE

She was running through the halls of the Academy. The halls were buzzing with the news—the pirate Tauron Ball had been captured. Her heart was in her throat, her mind turning over ten thousand scenarios for getting from the Academy to D-882.

"Lyssa!"

She spun around on her heel, and her heart stopped.

The Arch of Eron, the passageway for good souls to ascend to heaven, stood before her as it had in her childhood visits to Leveman's Vortex with Sostas, the silvery veil floating in the non-existent breeze. This was where she and her father would come to tempt fate and the Great Creator's will. This was where she first learned she was a bad soul.

But her eyes focused on the figure standing in the center, a rope around his neck.

"S-Sage..." She tried to run towards him, but her legs wouldn't move. She struggled more, needing to get to him, needing to save him from what she had done.

What she'd done?

"You did this." Lizbeth was next to Sage on the dais, her face accusatory and menacing. "You could have put Jukin away when you had the chance."

"I didn't...it's not..."

"You were stupid. Weak."

She spun around and found herself face to face with Jukin.

"Impatient. Petulant. Selfish."

Now Jukin was starting to sound like Sostas, and his words cut Lyssa to the core.

"*Cannot follow simple directions.*"

Was it the right thing to do?

"*I am about finished with you.*"

A loud boom of thunder echoed through the sky and her eyes fell as the ground crumbled around her. In front of her black boots, a jagged crevice appeared, red hot and steaming. She could see it, the river of fire, but she was in no danger of falling.

No, the crack was splitting the earth, headed towards the dais where Lizbeth and Sage stood.

"No!"

She gasped as she awoke, her eyes taking a moment to focus on the sunlight streaming across the ceiling. It took her a moment to remember where she was. Lizbeth's parents' house, in one of the two beds in the guest room. The other bed was already empty, but Lizbeth's personal belongings had taken up nearly three quarters of the room.

Lyssa rolled over to look out the window at the tall pine trees and let her mind wander back to her dream. The thought of Jukin arresting Sage was strangling and terrified her more than she expected it to.

Perhaps because it was intermingled with the guilt of knowing that if it were to happen, it would be her fault.

There was some part of her—the same one that felt responsible for Jukin—that excused all of his behavior. In that warped part of her brain, she knew that he was simply reacting to Sostas' abandonment and he couldn't possibly have been in his right mind when he had Tauron killed or plotted the assassination of the president. In her mind, it was all some big ploy for attention, hoping that he'd make a big enough name for himself that Sostas would return with a big ol' "attaboy, Jukin."

But that part of her brain ignored the larger danger—Jukin was still a free man. And he had killed before, and could kill again. Had she done the right thing in letting him walk?

The dream echoed in her mind again and she rolled over.

She and Sage had never spoken about when Tauron died. After it happened, she showed up later at Harms' bar and then spent the next week at his apartment with Sage. She'd cried then—the second and last time she'd done so in front of Sage—but he said nothing to her about what transpired or how he felt about it.

His words the night before were vulnerable and honest, and in the privacy of the empty room, she admitted to herself that it had frightened her. Sage was always steady in her mind —a steady pain in the ass, but steady nonetheless. Kind of like Harms, he was someone she could always count on to be where she needed him (even when she didn't want his help). She seemed to be the one who was always in need of support, but in that brief moment, Sage had been the weak one.

Unbidden, the dream came back into her mind, and she pictured that same, vulnerable look on his face as he stood on the dais at Leveman's Vortex. She rubbed her face again, trying to remove the memory, but it stayed firmly in place, along with a chorus of questions in her mind wondering if she did the right thing in letting Jukin go.

The scent of bacon reached her nose and she put aside her moral quandary for another sleepless night.

She padded down the stairs barefoot, still in her pajama shorts and tank when she heard hurried whispers at the foot of the staircase.

"You need to tell her." Lizbeth was using her no-arguments voice.

"Seriously, man, it's getting embarrassing." Ganon was there too, but who were they talking about?

"First of all, it's neither of your business." Sage was the target of their advice, and he sounded none-too-pleased about their unsolicited overtures.

"She's my friend," Lizbeth argued. "And she deserves to know."

"And I'm sure you can guess how she's going to take it," Sage snarled back.

"Yeah, I wonder how Lyssa's going to take it," said a voice behind her. She scowled and looked up at Sobal, who stood at the top of the stairs.

Immediately, the three voices quieted.

Lyssa completed the trek down the stairs and saw Lizbeth and Ganon looking as if they had been caught. Sage, however, had flushed bright red.

"Tell me what?" Lyssa asked.

"Weren't talking about you," Lizbeth said definitively. "Quit eavesdropping."

"*Breakfast!*" Billie called, effectively ending the discussion as the group high-tailed it to the table to have their meal.

Curiosity began to eat Lyssa alive as she pondered what the three of them could have been whispering about. The obvious answer was herself, but what in particular did they know that she didn't? As she nibbled on her toast, she determined it must be connected with why she couldn't have her mini-computer. The "detoxing" excuse was just that—an excuse—and Lyssa didn't buy it for one second.

"What are you plotting over there?" Lizbeth asked, narrowing her eyes at Lyssa.

"Nuffin'," Lyssa said around a mouthful of toast.

"That's right, nuffin'," Lizbeth snorted.

The breakfast conversation quickly turned to the plan for the day. Joe was already out on the dock, preparing the boat for the day trip out on the lake. Lyssa barely finished her breakfast before Lizbeth dragged her upstairs to get ready.

"Don't worry, I made sure to pick something up for you to wear," Lizbeth said, digging in her dresser drawers and pulling out a plastic bag. She tossed it over to Lyssa with a devilish grin.

Lyssa opened the bag and pulled out two small pieces of cloth.

"Um..."

"It's darling, and you will wear it," Lizbeth said in that same no-arguments tone.

"I'm not wearing this."

"Put it on."

"Lizbeth—"

But Lizbeth had already disappeared into the adjacent bathroom to put on her own suit. Lyssa grumbled and took off her pajamas, sliding the waterproof material over her skin. She focused on her reflection in the mirror, the way the cups in the top pushed her breasts up, the way the black stretchy material—

There was a knock at the door.

"Yo, are you ready?" Ganon's voice floated through the door and Lyssa suddenly panicked at the thought of walking out without any clothes on. Sage and Lizbeth, she had no problem with. But Ganon was a veritable stranger.

"Oooh!" Lizbeth appeared in the doorway in a bikini that was mostly string and left little to the imagination. Her curly hair was pulled up into a messy ponytail that fell down her shoulders. She eyed Lyssa up and down.

"Please let me wear something else," Lyssa pleaded, covering her chest with her arms. "Please."

"*Fine!*" Lizbeth pulled a huge white t-shirt from the drawer and handing it over to Lyssa who pulled it over her head and relished in being a little more covered.

They bounded down the stairs to join the rest of the group who were putting coolers and various floatation devices onto the boat. The lake before them was vast, the far side of the beach barely visible across the glassy water. Joe commented that it was a good day for boating, whatever that meant. But since this was their private lake, they would be the only ones out on the water.

Once the boat was ladened with more stuff than Lyssa ever thought could be needed, they set off in the tiny white vessel. The wind whipped around her hair, which soon became salty with the splash of water every time a wave splashed the side of the boat. They came to the center of the lake and Joe slowed the boat, the nose of the vessel dipping lower as the engine cut off. They bobbed in the wake they'd created for a moment. Sage helped Joe lower two anchors to keep them stationary, and Lizbeth began tossing the inner tubes into the water. Ganon wasted no time, diving in and climbing onto one with a wide, relaxed grin on his face. Sobal followed, albeit a bit clumsier on his descent into the water.

Sage appeared next to Lyssa on the bow of the boat with an armful of beer in cans. He tossed them to Ganon and Sobal, who caught them with some difficulty from their perch on top of the floats. He paused and pressed one icy can into Lyssa's hand without another word.

She held onto it and turned around to lean against the cushioned seat of the boat. Lizbeth was rubbing sunscreen into her skin, and talking with Joe, who was doing the same. Lyssa noticed the ease with which they conversed, the smiles on their faces. Joe touched Lizbeth's ear, rubbing in some sunscreen that she'd left there and she rolled her eyes at him. But there was nothing but affection there.

She shifted her attention to Sage, who pulled off his shirt and took the sunscreen from Lizbeth to cover his skin. Lyssa was a little transfixed by his ministrations and the way the muscles in his back moved with each stroke. He handed the tube to Lizbeth, asking her to put some on his back. Something akin to jealousy quietly nibbled at her in the back of her mind and she cracked open the can, downing nearly half of it in one gulp.

"Yo! Toss down some more!" Ganon called from the water. Lyssa peered over the edge of the boat, but Joe was faster, tossing three cans each to the two below. With a friendly grin, he handed another one to Lyssa and then to Lizbeth, and then to Sage, who declined with a smile.

Joe offered the beer again, a bit more forcefully, and Sage held up his hand in refusal. He rubbed the back of his neck and Lyssa noticed a hint of a blush rise up his neck. Lizbeth intervened, calling off her father and apologizing to Sage for his forwardness. Joe shrugged and cracked open the beer for himself and sat on the captain's chair in front of the steering wheel, a satisfied smile on his face.

Lizbeth jumped into the water, paddling over to Ganon, who seemed pleased to have her join him. But Sage walked the short distance to the front of the boat and plopped down next to Lyssa.

"Hey," he said, nudging her slightly. "What's up? You keep looking at me weird."

"Nothing," she snapped, hating that he'd caught her staring at him. "Didn't sleep well."

"Bad dreams?"

She turned to look at him sharply, wondering who told him and whom she needed to murder. When she recalled *she* hadn't told anyone about her dream in the first place, she relaxed a little. "Just didn't sleep."

"So about last night," he said, leaning back in the cushions and closing his eyes, "sorry I lost it for a little bit."

She folded her arms over her chest, still covered in the white t-shirt and hoped her face wouldn't betray her. "Yeah, well, you need to teach Sobal how to read a room."

"Don't be snippy today."

"I'm not being snippy! I just have a lot on my mind right now."

"You should have nothing on your mind right now other than enjoying yourself."

"Why is everyone so damned focused on whether or not I'm happy?" she barked, louder than she meant to.

"I give up." Sage stood and jumped into the water with a loud splash. The boat rocked for a moment from the force, and she glared at him over the side.

*Drip-drip-drip.* Ganon stood in front of her, a stern look on his face. "You're being a real piece of work after all that we've done for you so far."

"I didn't ask for you to drag me here," she growled at him, "so don't—"

Before she knew what was happening, Ganon yanked her up into his arms and tossed her over the side of the boat. She let out an ear-piercing scream before she hit the water hard, doused in the refreshingly frigid water of the lake. She sunk for a moment, stunned, before kicking and paddling herself to the surface, breaching it with a loud gasp of air.

Ganon smiled from the edge of the boat and tossed a beer down to the water.

"Now, how's about you swim over to those inner tubes, drink your beer, and adjust your attitude so you don't ruin the entire day with your saltiness?"

Chastened, Lyssa swiped the beer out of the water and swam over to Lizbeth and Sage.

***

Boating, as it turns out, was the most amazing thing Lyssa had ever done in her entire life. Or at least it felt that way after about three beers in the hot sun. She'd lost her modesty and the white shirt, and lay sprawled out in the black inner tube with one hand clamped around a warming beer and the other lazily dipped in the cool water.

She could barely remember what she was worried about earlier in the day, relishing in this contented feeling with her closest friends.

"You okay there, Lyss?" Sage asked, lying on his stomach on a tube next to her with his hand on her other foot. He squinted at her with one eye open.

"Yep."

"Good," he said, squeezing her foot. She smiled at his touch.

"Oi! Any of you want another one?" Ganon called from atop the boat. Lyssa and Lizbeth waved, as did Sobal from the other side of Sage.

A shadow flew across Lyssa's face as Sage caught a can and cracked it open. With a heave, he leaned across her and switched out the fresh can with the half empty one. He poured the warm beer into the water, and she snorted.

"Can't do that," she said, slipping lower into her inner tube. "'s against the rules."

"What rules?" Sage asked, tossing the empty can up to Ganon on the boat.

"Academy rules. No littering." She sank lower in the tube, and dipped her fingers in the water again. "They'll revoke my license."

"Yeah, I've always wondered what you actually do at the Academy," Sage said. Their conversation was momentarily interrupted by Ganon jumping into the water. He swam over to Lizbeth's tube and clung to the edge.

"What are we talking about?" he asked.

"Lyssa's gonna tell us all about her fancy diploma," Lizbeth said, raising a lazy hand to play with Ganon's fuzzy dark hair. "And her Academy work."

"So you really have a diploma?" Ganon asked. "I thought that was just a cover."

"I seriously have a piece of paper that proves I graduated from the Planetary and System Science Academy," Lyssa insisted. "And I seriously work there from time to time."

"I saw it, I was there when she sold a planet," Lizbeth chimed in.

"Okay, so when you go to these planets," Sage asked, his hand still encircling her ankle. "What do you actually do?"

"She basically just walked around and tested plants," Lizbeth said. "Ran around a bunch."

"Yeah," Lyssa grunted at Sage, kicking her foot a little in his hand. "Why didn't you bring me running shoes?"

"Why do you need running shoes?"

"To *run*."

"She's insane, I tell you," Lizbeth said. "She runs for fun."

"Huh," Sage said, watching her thoughtfully. "That actually makes sense. You do run away *a lot*."

Lyssa couldn't find it within herself to be angry, but she tossed her empty beer can at Sage's head.

"I thought you said no littering, Lyssa," Lizbeth said. Sage fished the can out of the water and tossed it up into the boat.

"But I'm actually interested in this planet stuff," Ganon said. "So like...would you sell a planet like this?"

Lyssa looked around and shrugged. "I don't normally mess with D-planets. Mostly X- and B-planets."

"There's a difference?" Ganon asked.

"Good God in Leveman's, don't they teach you anything in school?" Lyssa huffed.

"Well, he didn't go to school, so..." Sage chuckled, especially as Ganon scowled at him. "So, Dr. Peate, what can you tell us about this planet?"

"Well, if I had my mini-computer—"

A chorus of groans echoed up from the other innertubes and Sobal laughed from far away. "Pay up, everybody!"

"Really?" Lyssa said, lifting her head up from the tube.

"You guys are still taking bets on that?"

"Their optimism is adorable," Sobal said with a devilish grin.

"So I can't even say the word?"

"Wait, wait, wait," Ganon said, holding up his hands. "What was the context of the mini-computer?"

Lyssa scowled. "I was going to say, if I had my mini-computer, I could tell you everything there is to know about this planet."

"Hah!" Sage barked, pointing at Sobal. "Non-pirate related statement. Out of bounds."

"This is ridiculous," Lyssa said with a grin that said she wasn't truly upset by it all. "I don't appreciate you three taking bets on my behavior."

"But when it's so predictable, how can we not?" Sobal shrugged.

Lyssa laughed, truly laughed, with the rest of the group, and even joined them as they made bets on each other and drank their way through their beer supply. Lyssa realized about midway through the afternoon that she was actually having a very good time. When she admitted as such to Lizbeth, a great celebration rang out from the group, the loudest from Joe.

They didn't return until all the beer was gone, and the sun was starting to hang low in the sky. After docking, Sage carried a passed-out Sobal off the boat while the rest stumbled drunkenly back up to the house. Lyssa and Lizbeth headed straight to their room, where Lizbeth crashed on the bed and was out immediately. Lyssa, however, was wide awake, and after a shower, decided to explore a little.

She quietly shuffled down the hall, pausing at the only other room on this floor where the guys had ruthlessly made their claim. Ganon was facedown in one of the beds, and Sobal was snoring loudly from a pile of clothes on the floor. Sage, still sober as he hadn't had a drop to drink on the boat, was probably down entertaining Billie and Joe.

She was about to turn out of the room when she noticed an electrical cord. She followed it from the outlet on the wall to a pile of clothes on the nightstand. With a slightly drunken grin, she sauntered over to the cord and tugged on it. Pushing aside the pile, she saw Sage's mini-computer alit with the charging symbol.

"Jackpot."

She unplugged it and settled on Sage's bed, a grin on her face.

On the other bed, Ganon snorted and she jumped a few feet. He flipped over and scratched his bare chest, his mouth opening as he snoozed on. She turned back to Sage's mini-computer and turned it on, ready to finally see the damage—

*Locked*

*[]-[]-[]-[]-[]*

Lyssa hissed and put the mini-computer to her chest. Ganon snorted again and turned his head to face her, and she saw a trickle of drool drop from his mouth. She picked up her head and looked at the floor, where Sobal was sleeping soundly, his skin rapidly turning red from sunburn.

She snuggled in deeper into the bed and stared at the empty boxes, trying to piece together what Sage would use for a passcode. She chewed on her lip and typed:

*1-2-3-4-5*

*Access denied*

Well, she should give him a little more credit than that. So she tried his birthday.

*Access denied. One try remaining.*

Closing her eyes, she pictured all of the different things about Sage that would inform her of his passcode. Obviously, piracy, bounty hunting—these didn't seem to be the phrases that defined him. Or really, a phrase he would use to protect his data. Something—or someone that he trusted. Ganon was an option, but that didn't seem like something Sage would do. Tauron was too long, and none of the other crew members were—

She popped open her eyes and smiled.

*7-2-9-4-2*

*R-A-Z-I-A*

But before she confirmed the entry, she paused. It was pretty obvious that she was Sage's friend, so that might not be a really good passcode—easy to break.

But…

*5-9-7-7-2*

*L-Y-S-S-A*

The computer switched on, showing her the breadth of applications at Sage's disposal.

"Am I good, or am I good?"

She cackled to herself as she found the pirate web application and the phone auto-logged her in.

She put the mini-computer to her chest and felt her

heartbeat. She knew what she was going to find, the icy dread swimming in the bottom of her stomach was proof of that. But she needed to know, she needed to see it in person and then she'd be able to accept it and move forward.

She typed in the phrase "Razia" and held her breath.

***

"*You son of a bitch*!" she screamed, after nearly flying down the stairs. She hurled the mini-computer across the room at the object of her ire. Sage ducked just in time as his mini-computer exploded on the wall behind him.

"Lyssa, what in Leveman's?" Sage stood up slowly. But her screams awoke the rest of the house, and they all thundered down the stairs in varying stages of sobriety.

"Lyssa, what's wrong?" Lizbeth asked, grasping her head in pain. "Too loud for—"

"Ask him, *ask him what's wrong*!" Lyssa seethed, barely able to speak coherently.

"She found my mini-computer," Sage said, picking up the now destroyed piece of equipment. "I hope you're planning to pay for this."

"Told you ya should have gotten it insured," Ganon piped up from behind Lizbeth.

"How could you lie to me?" Lyssa barked.

"I didn't lie about anything—"

"You kept the truth from me, same thing!"

Lizbeth piped up behind her. "It is definitely not the same thing."

Lyssa whirled around, her anger soaring even higher. "You knew?"

"Of course I knew," Lizbeth spat, not even the slightest bit afraid. "But what good was it going to do, you sitting around here bitching and moaning the whole time? At least I got you to relax for a day."

"*The last thing I need to do is relax!*" Lyssa screamed. "And all this time, I should have called Dissident."

"It's not gonna do any good," Ganon commented with a disinterested look.

Lyssa's eyes widened and she stared at him wordlessly before her fury overtook her and she advanced toward him. But Sage stepped in front of her, drawing her anger back to him.

"Ganon, you aren't helping," Sage snarled at him. "Lyssa, we'll fix this, I promise. I'll even help—"

"Oh, like you helped by dragging me to the middle of nowhere?"

"I don't understand," Joe said, looking between the four of them. "What happened?"

Lyssa's shoulders slumped and she closed her eyes, defeated.

"I'm back on probation."

# CHAPTER SIX

| | |
|---|---|
|  | N/A) (No last name listed), Razia |
| Wanted for | N/A |
| Reward | N/A |
| Known Alias | None |
| Known Accomplices | Tauron Ball, Sage Teon |
| Pirate Web Affiliation | Dissident* (probationary) |

| | |
|---|---|
|  | 17) (No last name listed), Razia<br>Captured by Jarvis Loeb. |

She stared at the capture record and bounty poster on her mini-computer, now returned to her possession. There hadn't even been an argument to cut their "vacation" (she scoffed) short, the pure rage radiating off of Lyssa had been warning enough that dissent would not be tolerated. Once back on Sage's ship, Lyssa had holed herself into Sage's room while the owner stood outside the door and apologized for over an hour. She ignored his overtures and soon he gave up. None of his crew bothered to see her off when they dropped her off at a transport station, but she was glad for it. Lyssa could barely stand to be in the same universe as all of them.

The transport station station was loud and boisterous and full of people in stupidly obnoxious good moods. One such gentleman had the audacity to sit next to her and comment on the good day he was having, but one intense glare was enough to silence him for the rest of the ride to the Academy.

Once she got to her ship, she wasn't quite sure what to do, but for some reason she set a course for D-882.

She knew she would have to make the call soon, but she had wanted to be alone in her ship when it happened. No use in having an audience for her impending humiliation.

She looked up at the screen again, the word "probation" mocking her. When a bounty hunter first joined the web, they had to ask permission to hunt pirates until they proved their mettle. Most of the time, it was a matter of weeks. It was rare—no, unheard of—for a pirate to suddenly go from the top twenty to probation.

But she wasn't most pirates, was she? The unfairness of it all was infuriating.

With a deep, calming breath, she pressed the "call" button on her dashboard and waited, steeling herself for the inevitable.

"What do you want?" Although Dissident was never happy to see her, today he seemed, if possible, even more disgusted by the sight of her.

She decided to cut right to the chase. "So, how long until I'm off probation?"

"How long? *How long*? You are *lucky* that you remain in my web at all. Highly embarrassing to be captured. You *know* better."

She bit her tongue, not wanting to make the situation worse by arguing with him. Other pirates get captured every day, but that argument wouldn't fly with Dissident. He seemed pretty entrenched in his opinions of her and no matter what she said to him, he wouldn't listen.

Instead, she swallowed and asked, "So then who am I allowed to…hunt now?"

"Humph. Ask me again in a few weeks."

"No!" she exclaimed, terrified that he was going to give her the run-around for six months, like he did when she first joined the pirate web. "Dissident, I swear, don't pull this shit with me again."

"You are in *no place* to give demands," he seethed. "And if you try and threaten me again, I'll have you arrested the next time you set foot on D-882."

"Give me *somebody*," Razia pleaded.

"Fine…you can take Akiva Bienes." Dissident barely got the words of his mouth before the call ended.

She repeated the name in her head, unsurprised that it did not ring a bell. When she was on probation the first time, Dissident took joy in giving her the most obscure pirates he could find. Her question now was how bad it was going to be.

| | |
|---|---|
|  | 1000) Bienes, Akiva |
| Wanted for | Engagement in piracy, Petty theft, Burglary |
| Reward | 40C |
| Known Alias | None |
| Known Accomplices | None |
| Pirate Web Affiliation | Protestor |

"Son of a *bitch*!" she screamed, standing up and pacing around her bridge.

The last person on the bounty list?

There were other pirates worth less, of course, but the actual bounty list only numbered up to one thousand. When she'd been on probation the first time, she'd worked Dissident up to the seven hundreds at least.

And now she was back at square one.

Because she wasn't worth any better.

She let out a shaky breath, the thought entering her mind unbidden and unwelcome. For as much as she had felt like her life was going well, in the bottom of her soul, she had been waiting for the bottom to drop out. Because no matter how far she had come, no matter how much she pretended otherwise, she still knew that the Great Creator wasn't going to let her be happy. She didn't deserve good things that others received. While she swaggered and boasted about her new status as a top pirate, she knew in her heart it was just an act.

She had been dreading the moment when her bounty would disappear, and because she had been stupid and stubborn, she hastened her own demise.

A dam broke in her mind and she began to think back to every conversation with Harms, every time she argued with Sage. And then, painfully, every time Tauron would drag her back to the Academy, ordering her to stay there. She'd been so eager to escape a life as Lyssa that she'd been blind to the reality as Razia. And now, with the cold, hard truth staring her in the face, she could avoid neither.

Was it time to just accept her fate and hang up her boots?

The answer did not come as easily as she wanted it to.

***

"Ah, haven't we been here before?" Harms smiled at her as she slunk into his booth, defeated. She wasn't there to ask for his help; there was no need for that. And she wasn't really there to get an idea of the current pirate climate regarding her reputation, although that was the excuse she made for herself. Rather, she just needed to see a kind face and get a little bit of sympathy.

Harms, however, seemed to find it all highly amusing. "So, you've had an eventful few days. How was jail?"

She glared at him and shook her head.

"Did you have a good vacation then?" His eyes glittered. "Heard you got to go on a boat of all things."

She couldn't help the eye roll as she replied, "Oh, it was fabulous. Just a riot. Does everybody know then?"

Harms chuckled. "Calm down. Nobody's really talking about it."

"About...any of it?"

"Nope. Most everyone's talking about this Pirate Ball."

She slumped lower in the booth. At least if they were talking about her capture, they'd be talking about her. But not to be in the conversation at all was terrifying. It's like they'd forgotten about her already. The mountain she'd have to climb (again) seemed insurmountable.

"Cheer up, Raz! Did Dissident at least give you someone to hunt?"

She nodded, her tongue stuck to the roof of her mouth. "The last guy on the list."

"Well, he's consistent, I suppose."

Anger burned inside her. "How is this funny to you?"

"Calm down," Harms tutted at her. "I know you're pissed off, but don't take it out on the people who are on your side."

She folded her arms tighter across her chest and glowered so she wouldn't say anything she regretted. She couldn't afford to torpedo this relationship again. She wasn't sure how many second chances Harms was willing to give her.

"Sorry," she muttered.

"So I take it you aren't here to ask for help, then?" Harms asked with a smile. "Shouldn't be too difficult to find him?"

"I haven't even started to look," she admitted, unfolding her arms. "Every time I start I just get..." She sighed heavily. No use in sugar-coating it for Harms. "Depressed."

Harms tilted his head and she was struck with the familiarity of this—her at his booth complaining about Dissident and him unable to help in any way but listening. Two years she'd suffered through this humiliation.

The question returned—was it worth it to keep going? She clenched her jaw to keep herself from asking the question aloud.

"Are you still on this planet, Raz?" Harms was waving his hand in front of her face. "You zoned out there for a minute."

"Yeah, I'm here."

"I know it looks bleak right now, but you figured your way out before, and I know you can do it again. Just play the game for a few weeks and maybe Dissident will change his mind."

The question of, "will he?" was on the tip of her tongue, but she couldn't ask it.

She couldn't reconcile paying for more than a few hours of parking on D-882, so she set off from Harms' bar to find her bounty. It wouldn't take her more than half an hour to find the guy. Because he was the last person on the list, he wasn't taking very many precautions. He didn't even have another alias to pay his apartment rent, so she knew exactly where he lived.

She grumbled and stuffed her hands in her pockets, kicking the dust up in anger. What would capturing this bounty prove? Dissident was just trying to get her to quit calling him all the time. He was just throwing her a bone. Perhaps he'd just make it easy on himself and give her the last guy all the time.

He'd wait her out. The question was whose determination was stronger—hers to be a top bounty hunter, or his to keep her out of the limelight.

At this point, she'd put her money on him.

"I'm *not* giving up," she insisted to herself, needing to hear the words aloud so she would believe them.

Her bounty had just bought food at a small cafe near his apartment, and she found him chowing down without a care in the world. He was pudgy, with nubby fingers shoving a huge sandwich into his mouth. Every few bites, he'd smash a handful of chips in after the sandwich, or take a long sip of his drink. As she got closer, her nose turned up in disgust; he smelled like he hadn't showered in days.

She sighed as she sidled up next to him with a bored look on her face.

"Whatchoo want?" Bienes grumbled between mouthfuls.

She forced herself to sound somewhat interested. "I'm here to capture you."

His mouth fell open, crumbs of his sandwich falling into his lap.

"Look, I don't like it any more than you do, and I'll even let you finish your lunch if you'll come—" He tossed his drink in her face and scrambled out the door.

She sat at the bar, her eyes burning and her face sticky with cola as she considered just how far she had fallen in that moment. She pushed herself off the bar and walked out after him. He seemed out of shape, so it wouldn't take long for her to catch him. She felt the cola seeping into her shirt, and grumbled, realizing she'd have to take him to the bounty office and make it all the way out to her ship on the outskirts of the city before she could get a clean shirt.

"Asshole."

She heard him before she saw him, panting in an alley

two blocks from the cafe. He was leaning on his knees, wheezing and puffing with exhaustion. When she approached him, she got a whiff of his terrible body odor.

"Leveman's!" She gagged, putting her hand over her face.

"Oh, come on!" he panted. "Not you. Anybody but you."

Her mood went from disinterested to furious in an instant. "And what is that supposed to mean?"

"Man, I won't hear the end of it. I got caught by the stupid girl—"

She reared her fist back and decked him, knocking him out cold before he could finish his statement. He fell backwards, eyes crossed, and lay splayed out in the alleyway. Hands shaking, she unclipped her floating canvas from her utility belt and tossed it on the ground. She held her breath as she bent down to him and rolled him onto her canvas, handcuffing him for good measure. The floating discs attached to each corner levitated upward, and she let out her breath, the smell of him still disgusting in her nose.

Grabbing the canvas' cords, she yanked him forward, praying that no one would be at the bounty office so she wouldn't have to suffer the humiliation.

***

Apparently, Razia had no luck.

The bounty office looked like Top Pirates on Parade, packed with at least twenty of the most well-known pirates. She steeled herself and walked to the back of the line, keeping her head down, hoping that she'd avoid attracting any unwanted attention.

Her bounty moaned as he awoke, turning and tossing

from side to side as he became aware of his surroundings. When he grew more lucid, his face contorted into one of disgust.

"Well, *this* is embarrassing," he announced loudly, and catching the attention of the nearby pirates, Conboy Conrad, a member of Insurgent's web, and, in cuffs, Olvire Gongago, who was part of Protestor's web. They completely ignored Razia as they struck up a conversation with her bounty.

"Yeah, bad luck for you, mate," Conrad said, peering down at him.

"The funny thing is, she didn't even try very hard," Bienes replied, craning his head to look up at Gongago.

"Shut up!" Razia hissed down at him.

"Well, of course she didn't," Gongago said.

Conrad snickered. "Probably didn't want to break a nail."

"I'm only worth a few hundred credits anyways, wasn't prepared for a bounty hunter to show up."

"Who would be?" Gongago said.

"*Knock it off!*" Razia barked.

"Who would ever send a bounty hunter after me? Then again, I guess her runner wants to keep her in her—*Oof!*" Razia's foot connected with his face. If she hadn't knocked him out, she at least hoped she'd broken his jaw so he couldn't speak anymore. But his eyes rolled into the back of his head, and he fell back onto the canvas.

Gongago and Conrad snickered at her loss of temper.

"You know, that's super bad for you," Gongago said, "getting hit in the head like that."

"I'm *sure* I don't care." She prayed the minutes would tick by faster, but the line remained unmoving.

"I told ol' Max Fried the other day, I says, it's only a matter of time before that girl gets caught."

Razia glared at Gongago. "Aren't *you* the one in handcuffs?"

"Yeah," he smirked. "But when I get out, I ain't on probation, like you are."

She muttered a very foul curse under her breath.

An eternity passed before Razia deposited her bounty at the window. The man on the other side seemed less amused to see her now than a week ago and was happy that she was only receiving a paltry forty credits for her work. She, on the other hand, was just relieved to get out of the torture chamber.

She ducked into the alley and closed her eyes, hoping that somewhere in the bottom of her soul, she could find the strength to continue on. If it was going to be like this forever—the low bounties, the snide remarks, the effort it took to get to D-882 to find a bounty, capture that bounty, bring them to the bounty office for a mere few credits…

And the question returned—was it worth it?

Was she worth it?

A noise drew her attention and she saw a familiar shape appear in the alley. For whatever reason, Relleck was a welcome sight. She even forgot about what he said to her at Eamon's.

"Hey," She smiled, but he didn't look too pleased to see her. "How ya been?"

"Have a good vacation?" he asked bitterly.

"How did you know about that?" Razia asked, but then answered her own question. "Harms."

"You and Sage, alone for a whole week."

"We weren't alone," Razia said. "His crew, and Lizbeth, and..." She chewed on the side of her lip. Relleck had been interested enough in her to make out with her a few times, maybe he was still interested enough to get her to come over to Contestant's web. After all, Dissident seemed to loathe her, but Contestant might be less concerned about her gender and more about the way she'd plucked off nearly every pirate in his web.

"So..." She swallowed. "As I'm sure you're aware, I'm back on probation."

He snorted.

"And I was wondering if maybe...you'd put a good word in for me with Contestant," Razia finished, feeling dirty for saying it at all. But she was getting a bit desperate.

"Really?" Relleck said with a sly grin. "You want me to get my runner to add you to his web? When you aren't even worth a single credit?"

"It's just a technicality," Razia said nervously. "It's only because no one put any—"

"And the only bounty on your head was that damned scientist," Relleck continued, clearly enjoying this, "which, in my book, means that you were just a fluke."

Razia's heart thumped in her chest, and it had nothing to do with his memory of Pymus. "I've captured every one of the top pirates—"

"Contestant doesn't need any more bounty hunters."

"Are you serious? We... I mean, you... I let you...and you won't help me?"

Relleck smirked. "I don't know what you think this—" he pointed between the two of them in the same way she had, "—was, but *that wasn't it.*"

Razia gaped at him. She was hurt and, at the same time, shocked at how much her own words thrown back in her face bothered her. "Relleck, I..."

"You can't have it both ways, Razia. Why don't you go ask your pal Sage for help?"

"Okay, really," she exclaimed, "*what* is it with you and Sage?"

"You know, for a while I thought you were just lying to me," Relleck said with a strangely sad look on his face, "but now I see that you're lying to yourself."

"...Again, what in Leveman's Vortex are you talking about?"

"See ya around."

"Relleck!" Razia called after him but he didn't turn around. She slumped against the wall, shocked and confused, and hurting somewhere in the bottom of her heart. She never really liked Relleck, but she thought maybe he would be a bit more helpful since she did let him kiss her, albeit in private and she had threatened him within an inch of his life if he told anyone.

But still.

Her back pocket buzzed. She pulled out her mini-computer and groaned loudly. As if things weren't bad enough.

"Yes, Dorst, what—"

"You know, Lyssa, I have given you a wide berth lately," Dorst began, his tone sounding like he'd been holding in this rant for a while. "I have allowed you to disappear for months at a time, no questions asked, because Vel tells me that you're doing good work. I've covered for you, I've excused you, I've done just about everything to protect you from the bureaucracy of the Academy. But now, now I need you to help me out."

"I—"

"I asked you to take our brother under your wing, to spend time with him," Dorst continued, cutting her off. "And yet, he's been here at the Academy without you for the past month."

"I haven't done any DSE stuff!" Lyssa sputtered, finally able to get a word in edgewise. "And besides, I don't know what you want me to do!"

"You can start by getting your ass back to the Academy and picking him up!"

"I'm really far away," Lyssa whined, although really D-882 was only three hours' hypermiling from the Academy.

"Get. Here."

# CHAPTER SEVEN

Lyssa arrived at the Planetary and System Science Academy a few short hours after her phone call with Dorst. She could have told her brother to buzz off; she could have continued to ignore him. But at the same time, there was a small Vel-sounding voice in her mind that pointed out Dorst hadn't been the worst supervisor. She couldn't remember the last time someone asked about Sostas' work, probably since Pymus, if she were being honest. And although he'd been bothering her for things like her licenses and physicals, that was coming more from the Academy than from him.

So, begrudgingly, she admitted to herself that she might owe it to him to make his job a little easier and not have him send the U-POL after her again.

She stepped onto her ship ramp and looked around the busy Academy docking station. Ships of all sizes filled the station, mostly research vessels big enough to hold the staffs and junior scientists of the more successful scientists.

She tried to picture herself with a staff. Considering the last two employees she'd had—one brother she had left on a planet and another brother she had left at the Academy for the past month—she wasn't sure she'd be any better with ones she wasn't related to.

She could throw Dorst a bone and take Heelin on an excavation, but that would mean she'd have to do it the old fashioned way—without the use of her father's proprietary sensors. He'd built them when she was a kid so she could gather data while he tinkered with his research on Leveman's Vortex. She rebuilt them from the schematics she found in his lab, thanks to Tauron's crew members who were much more adept at equipment building than she was.

The lift doors opened and she slowly walked down the long hallway, considering her years at the Academy. She snorted, considering the number of times she'd had to get creative to sneak out of the station, and, with a less amused smile, the number of times Tauron drug her back. Sage was right—it had taken a long time for Tauron to accept having her on his ship.

Again, she kicked herself for missing the signs. The look on his face when she found him on D-882 the first time should have been enough to dissuade her, but it only made her more stubborn. He had tried everything in his power to get her to remain at the Academy. He pretended to be her older brother to her professors, he tried bribing her with money. He tried reasoning with her the same way Sage and Harms and everyone else had all of these years.

Was she really that stubborn?

She looked at her mini-computer and wished Vel were there. He always seemed to know the right thing to say to her, even if she wouldn't admit it at the time. But he was far away on a deserted planet. She hoped he'd brought enough things to survive, unlike her three-month stint alone. That was true planetary survival, because she'd only expected to be there a night or two. She'd thought Tauron would come get her, but after a week of nothing, she realized Tauron wasn't coming. She'd yelled at him a long time for that when she returned.

"Damn it," she muttered.

She slowed her walk in a sort of Event Horizon-esque hope that the closer she got to the center, the slower time might pass, until she was infinitely never getting—

The doors to the lab slid open, and she was face to face with Heelin.

"Well, it's about damned time!"

She supposed she might have deserved that. "I'm here, I'm here," she muttered, stepping through the threshold into the lab. It was bigger than the one she'd inherited from Sostas. This one reeked of Serann money, and Sostas' was purchased before his widely-known marriage to the eldest of the Serann daughters. Even with their money, Dorst couldn't afford a lab of this size by himself, so he split the difference between siblings number four and seven—Hasidus and Kasan (Lyssa was thirteenth born from Jukin and Vel was a paltry sixteen in the long line of twenty-four siblings). Dorst was the eldest son still at the Academy, so he took it upon himself to hire the younger siblings who were still starting out, (except for her, of course). She noticed a couple of other blonds amongst the crowd of working scientists that could have also been her siblings or cousins.

She wondered if Jukin would have been so magnanimous if he'd remained in the Academy instead of ditching and becoming a police officer. Considering he didn't even recognize his own sister, she wasn't hopeful. She brushed aside her feelings about Jukin to remain stoic in the face of Hasidus and Kasan, who had joined her and Heelin in some kind of Peate family reunion.

"And here we thought we'd be done with you for good," Hasidus said with a sneer. He, at least, hadn't changed much.

"Your boss summoned me," Lyssa smirked, knowing that it would push his button.

Like clockwork, Hasidus bristled but Kasan spoke instead. "It's about time. You've been gone for months. Do you know how many times scientists have stopped in and asked for you?"

"Why would they want anything to do with me?" She couldn't fathom why, unless...

"Obviously, people are still very interested in Father's work," Hasidus said, finding his tongue again. "And your disappearing doesn't help things."

"I haven't heard..." Again, she realized how blissfully unbothered she'd been, no one had accosted her in the hallway, no one had sent her any nasty messages (that she'd seen, in any case). She supposed she'd just assumed that was because Pymus had disappeared, but was someone actually just keeping the deluge of curiosity from her?

The door opened and Dorst walked through, looking less angry than when he called her. He handed the file he was holding to Hasidus, who took with just a hint of disdain before handing it off to Kasan, who began thumbing through it. Dorst then looked to Lyssa and clamped his hand down on her shoulder forcefully, as if she'd run away if he let up, and he didn't relinquish his grip on her shoulder until she was seated in front of him and his office door was closed.

"You wanted to see me?" Lyssa asked, feeling a little nervous.

"About thirty times since you became my subordinate," Dorst said with a tight smile. "But no matter, you're here now and we have a lot of things to discuss."

"Surprised you didn't send the U-POL after me again," Lyssa muttered, relaxing a little bit and sitting back.

Dorst snorted and pulled a thick file from his desk drawer, thumping it down on his desk.

"What's that?" she asked nervously.

"Your file," Dorst said, flipping through each page with an unreadable expression on his face. "Discipline reports, overdue license renewal notices, missed appointments with me—you know, the usual litany of paperwork for a certified Deep Space Exploration scientist."

Lyssa shifted uncomfortably.

"And, of course, inquiry after inquiry from the DSE board. 'Where is she? Why hasn't she presented her findings on Leveman's Vortex?'"

"I'm...not finished with it yet?" Lyssa tried. Leveman's Vortex had been so far from her mind (with the exception of her foul language) that she was out of practice lying about it.

"To be honest, I could give a shit about that stupid black hole," Dorst said. "And whatever Father had you doing, or you continue to do, is your business."

Lyssa blinked at him, shocked. Not even a year ago, when he'd found out that Vel was interning with her, he'd sneered, "Don't think this will change anything" and could barely stand the sight of her. And now he was saying that he had little to no interest in what she was up to? Not even to ask about Sostas?

"I really can't spend half my time covering for you," Dorst finished, sounding exasperated. "You need to make a decision, Lyssa. Are you going to be a DSE or are you going to do...whatever else it is that you do with your time?"

"I..." The question caught her off guard, as it had been the one bouncing around in her head. As Razia, she struggled to get even a few hundred credits added to her name, but at the Academy she could make a name for herself. She could share Sostas' work with the UBU. Even if she just patented his sensors, she'd make more money than her inheritance and bounty hunting income combined. She was boxed into this life of mediocrity and embarrassment as Razia and it would be so simple to just give it up.

But planet excavation and scientist glory wouldn't bring her the kind of joy capturing a bounty brought. She was still addicted to the idea that she could find that glory as Razia, no matter how much she felt like she was screaming into a vacuum.

"Don't answer now," Dorst said with a small hint of a smile, "because now, you are paying me back for all the bullshit I've had to take care of for you by taking care of Heelin for me."

"Fine." She sat back, glad that they were off her life choices discussion. "So what, just take him on a couple of excavations?"

"I honestly don't care about that," Dorst said, surprising Lyssa even more. "What I need you to do is just spend some time with him. I think he needs a course correction."

"I don't follow."

"Well," Dorst sighed, pulling off his glasses, "I was hoping that you would be able to inspire him to quit the Academy."

Lyssa wasn't sure which shocked her more: that Dorst thought Heelin needed to quit or that he was asking *her* to help. "W..what?"

"Whatever it is that you do on your…down time," Dorst said, giving her a sly look, "Vel's always talking about how happy it makes you, and that I shouldn't press you to be here more than the minimum."

"Oh," Lyssa said, torn between affection toward Vel and shame at her own failures.

"And so, I thought that you'd be a good influence on Heelin, get him to realize that he's not happy doing planet excavations with me, and that if he wants to…well, follow his dreams, he should."

"What's stopping him?" Lyssa surprised herself at her genuine curiosity.

"I think you can probably guess," Dorst said. "Starts with an 'm' and ends with—"

"Bitch."

"That is my mother you're referring to," Dorst warned.

Lyssa's last encounter with Mrs. Dr. Sostas Peate ended with the latter telling her, in front of the entire family, that she wished Lyssa had never been born. "So? Tell the old cow to buzz off and go do what you want."

"We don't all have your gumption, Lyss," Dorst replied. "Of all the Peate kids, you are the only one who doesn't give a crap what anyone thinks of them. The rest of us..."

"I'm not...sure of..." Lyssa shook her head. "I mean, I just...."

"Mother was furious when Jukin dropped out and became a police officer. But, as you know, he *always* gets a free pass, because he's the *first born.*" Lyssa was impressed with the jealousy Dorst displayed as he spoke. "And the rest of us, save you, have been too afraid to incur her wrath to step a toe out of line. But I think Heelin is...well, he's not happy here, I can tell you that. Mopes around all day, takes forever to complete a simple task."

"So, what does he want to do?"

"He won't tell me." Dorst shook his head. "If you ask him, everything is fine. But I did see an application to the Universal Police Academy on his desk once."

Lyssa gagged. "Heelin wants to be a police officer? Like... like..."

"Jukin, yes."

Lyssa wasn't sure she could handle two brothers in the U-POL Special Forces, especially since Heelin seemed a little quicker on the uptake. He might recognize her, given the opportunity. "And you…support this?"

"I think it would be good for Jukin to realize that he's not an island either. He barely comes home anymore—virtually never since the assassination attempt on the president last year. Mother's worried about him, but none of us can ever get to him since he's on that damned pirate planet all the time. I would like to have another one of us there with him to keep him company."

Lyssa stifled an ironic snort, but Dorst must have seen it.

"You're a lot like him, you know," he said.

That was enough. "I am nothing like that self-centered, egotistical—"

"That's what he said about you, too. You know, I went to go see him about your inheritance."

Her inheritance. It took all of her mental strength to keep her face from displaying the jumble of emotions buried underneath her skin.

"I told him to give it back to you, but unfortunately…" Dorst sighed heavily. "He said it was gone."

Used to pay for the potential murder of hundreds, maybe thousands of other pirates. She considered again that she'd not only stopped the plot and protected the pirates, but she'd also saved her wayward brother's ass all in one fell swoop. And the Great Creator thanked her by putting her back on probation.

She became aware that Dorst was looking at her, and she sniffed, trying to look uninterested. "I didn't need it, it would seem."

"That's the thing about you, Lyss," Dorst said. "Ever since you were a little girl, you've never needed anybody for anything. You know what you want, and you go after it. And I've yet to see you fail."

Except at being the universe's most wanted pirate. She'd been going after that pipe dream for three years with nothing to show for it.

"And that is why I thought making Heelin your assistant would be a good thing."

Lyssa again shifted in her seat, wondering when Dorst started to respect her, *admire her* even.

"I'll…try…" she said, and it was honest.

"Well, that's all that I had for you." Dorst paused and smiled. "Unless there was anything you needed to discuss with me…"

Lyssa didn't like his tone. "What are you talking about?"

Dorst leaned forward with a sparkle in his eye that was unfamiliar. "Curious about that guy who dropped your ship off here a few weeks ago…"

"That was nobody," Lyssa snapped, hoping against hope that Sage hadn't been too mouthy.

"Nobody?" Dorst asked, that stupid look still on his face. "Fine, fine. I'll just ask Vel about it when he gets back. Your friend seemed awfully pleased to meet me, you know. Said he was taking you for a week's vacation somewhere—"

"Yeah, we're done here."

***

*Stop making friends with all of my brothers, asshole.*

Lyssa walked out of Dorst's office, her fingers dancing over her mini-computer as she fired off the terse message to Sage. Her eyes landed on Heelin and she frowned. Vel would be better at this career-guidance thing than she, which was impressive considering he didn't have one in the first place.

She sidled up to Heelin, who looked even angrier than normal.

"What do you want?" he snapped, not looking at her.

"Dorst says we should work together."

Heelin snorted. "He's trying to teach us both a lesson and Leveman's if I know what it is."

"He wants you to follow your passion," Lyssa said, cutting right to the chase. "He thinks you aren't happy here."

"Is *anyone* happy here?" Heelin observed, looking around the lab. Lyssa couldn't help but agree with his assessment. All of the assistants and doctors had the same dead, soulless expression as they worked.

"So leave," she said.

"And do what, exactly?" Heelin slumped back in his chair. "Mother would cut me off if I left the Academy."

"You don't have any money of your own?"

"Of course I do, but…I can't imagine never going home again."

Lyssa rolled her eyes at his weak reasoning. "She's not going to cut you off." To Heelin's doubtful look, Lyssa added, "She's not going to be in charge of things much longer anyway. Sera's taking over soon, right?" Tradition dictated that the eldest daughter took over the estate when the youngest daughter was introduced to their idiotic society. Sostas had left twelve years prior, which meant the youngest daughter was nearing her teenage years. Though Sera was obsessed with making babies and praying, she didn't seem to have the lofty opinions of herself that Eleonora Peate had.

"Mother will never give up her seat at the head of the table. And even if she does, she's..." Heelin sighed. "She wants us all to toe the line. Except Jukin." He snorted. "Must be nice to be the first born and do whatever you want."

"I do whatever I want."

"Yeah, but you've always been headstrong. I mean, it's like something changed in you after you were kidnapped."

"Well, yeah, I—*wait a minute, you remember when I was kidnapped by Tauron*?" She nearly fell over with surprise. No one in the family, not her mother, not even Jukin, remembered that incident. It was a sore point with her, especially when she had "kidnapped" Vel the year before.

"I was *there*!"

Lyssa blinked at him, her mouth open. "You were?"

"We were in the same damn class!" he snarled, shaking his head. "That pirate showed up on that field trip and hoisted you over his shoulder, screaming and crying ..."

The day Tauron had kidnapped her was, at first, the worst of her life. He'd commandeered the Academy transport shuttle headed for one of the training planets for young scientists. He was looking for a Peate and somehow landed on her. She had been so terrified that she had blocked most of the events out, but Tauron told her later that she screamed and cried and fought him. The only other vivid memory was Tauron talking with Jukin, telling him that he had captured his little sister.

She could see it as clearly as she could see Heelin standing in front of her. Watching Tauron swagger in front of the screen, telling Jukin he'd better stop targeting pirates or else. And when Jukin called his bluff, Tauron swaggered over to her and pulled out a gun, pointing it at the space between her eyes.

*"Really? You want to kill* her*? Go ahead, be my guest."*

The memory stung as it replayed further. Tauron had called the Manor to see if he could at least get a ransom for her. But her mother had been similarly unwilling to help, telling Lyssa that if she was in so much danger, she should call her father. The father who had disappeared without a trace some months before.

She considered what her life might have been like if Tauron had chosen differently.

"You asshole!" she hissed, needing to slap him but refraining. "You let him take me instead of you!"

"I was twelve!" Heelin shot back. "What, do you think I could take on a fully grown pirate?" He paused and clenched his jaw. "But...I wish I could have stopped him. I was really glad when you showed up unhurt a few days later."

"I came back unhurt because Tauron was a good person." She remembered the fear when Tauron appeared in the doorway of the jail he'd stuck her in, and her shock when he sat down next to her and apologized for scaring her. He even showed her the gun and that it was unloaded. He explained that he was just trying to get a rise out of her brother. She remembered the way he rubbed the back of his head and grinned nervously, and the way his curls, gold-tipped and tightly coiled, bounced as he talked. He made her laugh through her tears, and for the first time, she knew what it was to be cared for.

"But you didn't..." Heelin trailed off for a moment, as if he wasn't sure he wanted to say it. "I mean, you didn't seem the worse for the wear."

"What?"

Heelin shrugged off her surprise. "I mean, you showed up at class the next week. You looked normal—determined, almost. You didn't talk about it, didn't even flinch about it."

"That's because..." Lyssa trailed off. Because she had made the decision to join Tauron's crew, to leave behind Lyssa Peate forever. But Tauron was determined *not* to let that happen. She had engaged in a battle of wills and schooling and the Academy were just distractions from the larger goal of becoming Razia. The memory of her stubborn insistence was striking in the light of what she knew now.

"Because you were working with Father, yeah," Heelin finished for her, off on his own train of thought. "I mean, it was clear that you weren't paying attention in class. I don't even know how you got such high marks all the time. We all just assumed Father was helping you with your homework."

"He wasn't. I mean..." She cleared her throat, not wanting to tell Heelin that she'd cheated her way through the Academy. "I don't know where he is. Still don't. Not since he left and—"

"I meant what I said. I don't care about him." Heelin sounded neither bitter nor upset, just matter-of-fact. "But you...whatever it was, it made you happy and you wanted to be doing it. And nothing and nobody could keep you from it. Every time I looked at you, you had your nose in your mini-computer." He sighed and looked a bit forlorn. "I wish I had that."

"Yeah, well...sometimes it's not all it's cracked up to be." Before she could answer Heelin's quizzical expression, her mini-computer buzzed at her hip. She looked down at it and sighed annoyed. "Hang on a second." She marched over to the corner and answered the call. *"What now?"*

"Wow, how about you try that again with just a *hint* less sass?" Lizbeth was sitting in her cubicle and looked like she hadn't slept a wink since their vacation at her parents' house.

Lyssa closed her eyes and took a deep breath. When she spoke, she pushed the words through a filter of niceness reserved only for Lizbeth. "What can I help you with?"

"I need you to come in for a deposition. General State wants your testimony to be public."

"No way," Lyssa said with a terse shake of her head. "I'm not getting up there and doing any more—"

"Lyssa, *please.*" There was no command in Lizbeth's tone, only a plea that sounded very unlike her. "I need you to do this for me. Trust me when I say I have tried everything in my power to spare you, but my hands are tied."

"I..." Lyssa swallowed her annoyed comment out of respect for her friend. "When?"

"Now."

"Sure, because I'm just around the corner."

"Oh hush. You're at the Academy, you can be here in a flash."

"...Did Sage give you a pirate web log-on or something?"

"Be at the Presidential Palace as soon as you can. Love you!"

The screen went dark as Lizbeth hung up, and Lyssa muttered angrily under her breath. The last thing she needed was to drop everything and go back to S-864. Dorst expected her to take Heelin with her wherever she was going, and she couldn't very well take Heelin to give a deposition.

But if it came down to pissing off Dorst or pissing off Lizbeth, Lyssa would take the former any day.

She walked back over to Heelin, who was doodling on the pad of paper he was supposed to use to document observations of the cell structure of the plant beneath the microscope.

"So...I have to go."

"Color me surprised."

"Trust me, I'd rather not, but...unavoidable."

Heelin turned to peer into the microscope again. She watched him, a part of her already out the door and another part urging her to stay. She sighed loudly and folded her arms across her chest. "Look, Heelin, I think if there's something that you want to do, you should do it."

Heelin snorted and didn't move to look at her.

"I mean, you can't live waiting to get approval from someone who is never going to give it." As the words came out of her mouth, she realized that she could have very well been giving herself advice about Dissident. But Eleonora wasn't holding Heelin's fate the way Dissident held Razia's.

"Are you done?" Heelin asked. "I have work to do."

She didn't appreciate his tone, especially since she was trying to do something nice for once. With a huff, she spun on her heel and stormed out of Dorst's lab.

# CHAPTER EIGHT

Razia's boots clacked against the stone streets as she strolled under a tall stone archway into the Presidential Square. The palace was the only remaining relic from a civilization long gone, and the clocktower, still on the old system of time, was minuscule and rickety-looking compared to the towering steel skyscrapers that surrounded it. The square also included the Universal Bank, a beautifully updated building with tall glass windows and a small area of wrought iron table and chairs for tourists to sit.

It was at these tables that Razia sat down, shivering in the mid-winter chill. She hated everything cold and made it her life's work to avoid any planets she needed to wear a jacket on. But if it was a choice between freezing in the cold or going inside the presidential palace, she was okay with being chilled.

When she'd been there the year before, the square was filled to the brim with people for President Llendo's victory speech. Her eyes moved over to the palace, and the balcony where Llendo had nearly died. If she squinted, she almost convinced herself she could see where the bullet ricocheted off of the stone ledge. Llendo had refused to let them repair it, saying it was an attestation to his legacy.

Her mini-computer lit up with Lizbeth's face. Razia grimaced at the reminder of her upcoming testimony, but made no move to get up. To keep Lizbeth off her tail, she fired off a quick message that she was nearby.

Part of her wanted to back out and disappear to a planet far away, but she knew that Lizbeth would spare no expense hunting her down.

She chuckled to herself, musing that at least she'd be wanted by someone. But her levity was short-lived, as reality washed back over her. She hadn't called Dissident since she had turned in her last bounty over a week ago, and he hadn't called her.

And if she were really being honest, she was rather hoping Dissident would just never call her again. Razia would fade into obscurity. Maybe fifteen years from now, Harms would be telling some new, young pirate about that one time—for a year—when there was a woman who was a pretty decent bounty hunter.

"Leveman's, this is sad," she whispered to herself.

"Well, my pants are firmly on my ass, as instructed."

Lizbeth's voice floated over the square. The wind blew her curls all over the place, and she hurried over in heels impossibly high.

"I believe I said I'll be down in a second," Razia retorted as Lizbeth sat down and wrapped her suit jacket tighter around herself.

"Look, this is a big deal for me," Lizbeth responded. "I need you to be...helpful today."

"I am going to be helpful. I've *been* helpful."

"You also need to be on your best behavior," Lizbeth said with a cautious look,"because this is going to be televised."

Razia nearly fell out of her chair. "Televised?"

"Yeah, didn't you know this entire trial has been all the rage here? We're getting higher ratings than the soaps."

"And if this is televised, then all the pirates are going to see it, too. Just what I needed: to remind them that I took a few billion out of their coffers. Because they already love me so much right now."

"I'm sorry," Lizbeth said, looking genuinely so. "And, for what it's worth, I'm sorry you're back on probation."

Razia bristled. "Are you also sorry that you lied to me?"

"No, I'm not, because we were trying to get you to relax," Lizbeth said with an exasperated look. "And you did, for a day. So I'll take that as win for you."

The warm day on the boat was a far off memory in the biting cold of the square and the weight of her probation problems. But she recalled a lovely day lazing on the lake with Lizbeth and Sage. A brief moment in time when everything was perfect and life was good. As usual, the Great Creator saw fit to destroy it all before she got too comfortable.

Lizbeth was waiting for Razia to respond so Razia allowed her a smile. "The boat was fun."

Lizbeth's face brightened and she looked less tired. "Dad can't wait for you to come back. He says he's going to teach you how to ski."

Razia laughed and shook her head. "That'll be a sight."

"But first, we need to go inside," Lizbeth said, pulling a hairbrush and some foundation out of her purse. "And you need to get ready."

Hair brushed and a little foundation applied ("For the cameras," Lizbeth had said), Razia followed Lizbeth through the maze of the presidential palace. They passed a hall with oil paintings of presidents past, each with the ominous clock tower and the palace looming over them. The hall was only big enough to show the last two hundred years of presidents, ending with Llendo's dimwitted smile hanging at the far wall.

They turned a corner, and Razia saw the television cameras ahead. Her heartbeat quickened. "Do I really have to do this?"

"Yes." Lizbeth turned to give her a reassuring smile. "It'll be just like you and I are having a chat. Ignore the rest of the circus."

The first camera spotted them in the distance and in a flash, they were surrounded by reporters and flashing lights.

"Razia, over here!"

"Razia, question for you!"

"Razia, is it true that there's more to the investigation than they're saying?"

"Smile and say nothing," Lizbeth said as her hand tightened around Razia's wrist. Lizbeth guided her through the throngs of people, both of them keeping their heads down and mouths closed. They entered into a large room that reminded Razia of a temple. Long pews lined either side of the walkway, mostly filled with people standing and talking. Lizbeth continued pressing forward to the front of the room as the media was left in the back. Lizbeth halted in front of a small table on the left of the room, facing a large elevated platform with several empty chairs.

Razia took a deep breath as she sank into the chair next to Lizbeth. She glanced back at the media behind her, still a mob of flashing lights and chattering conversation.

"Ignore them," Lizbeth said, looking through the papers on the table. "It's just a chat between the two of us."

"Uh-huh." Razia said, glancing back again. She scanned the faces of those sitting in the room and spotted Antica Mikaelsson, the smartly-dressed woman who had offered Lyssa Peate a job and was later found to be at least complicit in the illegal gun transfer. She was working out a plea deal to name names, although the only one she really had was Evet Delmur, who since he was immune to all criminal prosecution thanks to his membership to the webs. Razia was sure that explained the purple bags under Antica's eyes.

She scanned the room for the two masterminds of the conspiracy, Alfr Jos and Krishna Harmon, but didn't see them.

"They're in a real jail," Lizbeth explained after Razia asked. "You know, the ones that incarcerate people for more than a few hours."

"So they were convicted already?"

"Not quite, but they were denied bail thanks to their extensive connections with the pirates. Their trials will start after the investigation is complete."

"And when will that be?" Razia asked, curious only because it meant she didn't have to think about the chair with the microphone.

"After you give your deposition. We need to ensure that we've got…all the right people."

Razia swallowed but ignored the underlying comment in Lizbeth's response. "So when is this thing supposed to start?"

"Now," Lizbeth said, glancing up at the clock. "But General State is always late."

Razia began to chew on her lip. "General State? I'm talking to him today?"

"No, you're talking to me," Lizbeth said, ignoring Razia's concern. "He's just here as the senior officer in charge of the investigation."

General State knew Razia had lied about Jukin's involvement. Would he ask her about why she decided to spare him?

And what would happen if she came clean with the truth?

*All* of it?

"All rise!"

The doors swung open and everyone rose to their feet with a whoosh of air and movement. Lizbeth reached down and yanked Razia to stand as well, as the latter had remained seated in ignorance of decorum.

"Be seated, be seated," State murmured, his silver-rimmed glasses perched on his nose. He walked with the same sort of air as the first time she'd met him in the basement of the Presidential Palace. He took the empty seat in the center of the table and his aide handed him a folder of papers. He flipped through them, as the room remained silent.

He peered up over the rims of his glasses at Lizbeth. "Well?"

"Sir, this is the final deposition related to the assassination attempt of President Llendo," Lizbeth said, using a loud, curt tone. "As requested, today you will re-hear testimony of Razia, the bounty hunter who assisted me on the investigation."

"Yes, continue." State returned to his papers, but Lizbeth seemed to act like this wasn't anything new.

At Lizbeth's half-smile and nod, Razia stood slowly and made her way toward the podium. When she turned to sit, she took in the room, much fuller from this angle. At least twenty cameras pointed in her direction from the back of the room, and every eye seemed to be glued on her.

Including Jukin's.

She swallowed as she tried not to stare at him, sitting in the back corner with Opli next to him.

"Please state your name," Lizbeth said.

Razia opened her mouth to answer the question, but a camera flash blinded her. She began to answer "Razia," but then wondered how much longer she'd be able to use that name. When Dissident saw her bringing more attention to her involvement, he'd never take her call again.

"Razia," Lizbeth whispered quietly. "Please state your name for the record."

"Razia," she said, tossing her friend a thankful look. She supposed that her big reveal would be saved for another day.

"Any last name?" Lizbeth asked.

"None that I wish to share, thanks."

Razia saw the corners of Lizbeth's mouth twitch, and the warning glare to cut out the sass. Lizbeth continued with, "And what is your occupation?"

What was her occupation? She wasn't much of a bounty hunter now, taking the scraps given to her by Dissident.

If Razia didn't have bounty hunting, what did she have?

"Request a second, please?" Lizbeth said to General State, who nodded. She walked up to the stand and turned off the microphone. "Are you okay?"

"Yeah," Razia whispered.

"Seriously, you look like you're about to throw up," Lizbeth said.

"Agent Carter," General State's voice boomed across the courtroom.

"Sorry," Lizbeth said to him before quickly turning to Razia. "Take a deep breath. We're just talking, okay? Just focus on me and we'll get through this together."

Razia nodded. Lizbeth turned the microphone back on and adjusted her suit jacket.

"How did you get involved in the McDougall investigation?" Lizbeth said. "At first."

That was an easy question to answer, because they had rehearsed it many times before the first deposition. Razia spoke about the initial investigation, about the secret pirate meeting, about following the money from the diner (leaving out the piece about Mikaelsson, because she had that particular meeting as Lyssa Peate), to the guns on S-864.

"Explain how the guns made it from the arsenal on J-656 to S-864."

She spoke about Evet Delmur, and sunk back into her own mind as her words flowed out on auto-pilot describing how the gun running plot worked. In the back of her mind, she was considering a very different memory: the first time she'd met Delmur. She'd thought Dissident had given her a difficult pirate to hunt so she could prove herself to him. Turned out Delmur was simply overdue on his chocolate delivery to her runner.

She'd thought her life as Razia was over then, and if it hadn't been for a chance encounter with Opli and a case of mistaken identity, she might have. For a brief, glorious year, she had everything she wanted.

And then the Great Creator took it away.

She finished the story of the gun-running and how it tied into the conspiracy for the assassination: Secure Solutions, the shadow company set up by the Congressional Minister, would reap the rewards of an influx of new security contracts. That was, at least, part of the story.

"And was there anyone else involved in the assassination plot other than the players that you've named so far?"

Lizbeth's question was clear to Razia, whose gaze slid to Jukin. He was staring into blank space, a resolved nervousness etched on his face. She knew that he firmly expected her to tell everyone about his involvement.

And she wondered if she should.

A horrible, guilt-ridden thought slid through her head. If she told the truth, explaining that Jukin was not only complicit in this treason but he was planning to frame the pirate webs, that might be enough to sway Dissident to reinstate her as a full member of his web. She could make Jukin answer for everything he'd done and reclaim her own glory at the same time.

"Razia, please answer the question."

But when she looked at her brother across the courtroom, she didn't see a murderer, a conspiracist, nor an anarchist. She saw him at sixteen, when he'd come home from the Academy and heard that Sostas had taken her for his assistant. She saw pain etched on his face when he announced that he was going to quit his studies and join the U-POL—and she recalled with even more vivid clarity how her mother screamed and cried and blamed Sostas for it. But her father simply continued to eat his dinner, even as Eleonora's wails echoed in the dining hall. Lyssa and he left that evening for another months-long experiment at Leveman's Vortex, without so much as a goodbye to Jukin.

It was no wonder Jukin left her to die on that pirate ship. She might have done the same thing.

"No. No one else."

The room suddenly filled with sound and people and Razia was back on the stand, in the room, on camera. Lizbeth stood in front of her, General State stared at her from the raised podium, and she had just testified, under oath that no one else in the universe had been involved in this conspiracy.

"Thank you, Razia," Lizbeth said. "No more questions."

***

Razia didn't want to wait around for the rest of the hearing, so she slipped out a side door of the palace and into the alley. She leaned against the brick wall and sighed heavily, emotionally drained.

She wanted to forget any of this ever happened and return to her quiet life of...

Of what? Bounty hunting?

The weight on her shoulders grew heavier. Thanks to her televised appearance, she was fairly sure that she was out of the web now. And even if she wasn't, she was pretty sure that it was just a matter of time.

The door opened behind her, and she heard footsteps in the alley.

"Pirate."

Her heart stopped as she opened her eyes to stare at Jukin. They were alone in the alley, no lapdog, no Lizbeth. Just Jukin and...Razia, she had to remind herself. Jukin was looking at Razia, not his little sister.

He stared at her, and she caught a jumble of emotions etched on his face: exhaustion, curiosity, relief, anger. She stood to face him, taking in everything from his Universal Police uniform flecked with gold to the way his hands were fisted at his sides. He studied her in the same way, and he kept searching his eyes for a sign of recognition.

He stood in front of her for a long time before he spoke. "I knew about the conspiracy," he said, his eyes piercing hers.

"I paid for it, and I wanted to frame pirates for it."

"I know."

His brows furrowed and he shook his head, not understanding. "So why did you lie? Is this some kind of a sick ploy to blackmail me? Because, rest assured it will not work."

"Then why don't you tell the truth?" she asked, genuinely curious. "Do you really believe that killing the president was the right thing?"

"The plan was never to kill him," Jukin insisted. "At least, no plan that I was made aware of."

"But if the plan *was* to kill him, would you have still gone along with it? Would you have been able to live with yourself?" She stopped and swallowed hard. "Do you ever think about Tauron?"

"I…" His face turned thoughtful for a second, but then, as if realizing to whom he was speaking, he returned to anger. "That's none of your business."

She stepped forward but wasn't angry. "But it is my business, because I'm the one who saved your ass. I'd like to know if you truly are as big of a monster as I hope you aren't."

"Says the woman who kidnapped my sixteen-year-old brother at gunpoint."

"So you care about *him*, then? It bothered you that I kidnapped him? Threatened his life?" Razia asked, a little hopefully. Jukin might have done some terrible things, but at his core, he might've still been a good person. He cared about someone at least. Perhaps now he could begin to do the right thing and perhaps, for once, she didn't do the wrong thing.

"Of course it did, he's *family*," Jukin snarled. "He was a *kid*. And you…you will pay for what you did to my family. The same way Tauron did."

She was sure he meant this threats, and sure that she should have felt pain that he cared more for Vel than her. She was also sure she probably should worry about what he might do now that he was a free man.

But all she could think of was she needed to find a private place to process everything she'd just experienced.

And she needed a drink.

# CHAPTER NINE

*"No. No one else."*

"Can you change it?" Razia asked the bartender. He turned slowly to look at her up and down, but didn't move towards the monitor. So she had to choose between either watching her own pale expression on the screen or leaving. And since her whiskey glass was still mostly full, leaving wasn't an option.

She sipped more of it down and relished in the burn as she glanced up at the screen again. Her face was gone, replaced by some other story. But she'd seen her news story three times in the hour that she'd been there, so she knew she'd probably see it again.

She had been on her way to a planet to excavate so she

could disappear for a week, go for a long run. Somehow her ship parked in a docking station on the pirate planet, she'd taken an hour-long shuttle to the middle of the city, she'd sat at this bar, and she'd decided to drink away her problems instead.

Her mini-computer sat by her side, but the persistent, familiar urge to check it was gone. Dissident still hadn't called, and she wasn't about to call him either. No need in getting her hopes up just to have them dashed. She was getting tired of being disappointed.

She swallowed another gulp and sighed.

"So what, you're just going to sit here and get drunk, then?"

She grimaced as Sage slid into the seat next to her, ordering a water from the bar. "What do you want?" she asked.

"Well, since Vel isn't around to talk check on you, Lizbeth told me that I had to," he said with a smile. He eyed the image on the screen of her testifying and whistled. "You look like someone just ruined your birthday."

She glanced up, and swallowed more of her drink when Jukin appeared on the screen giving a statement.

"Any fallout from that inheritance fiasco?" Sage asked, giving Jukin a dirty look. "Did you ever get your money back?"

She shrugged, watching the ice clink in her glass as it melted. "Not really worth it."

"Seemed worth it at the time."

She winced, remembering her slow descent into hysterics

when she pulled the bank statement from the archives. "I mean...to get it back from him. Lizbeth said that whatever was left had been returned to him."

"So you're just going to let him walk away with five billion credits?" She heard the angry tone in Sage's voice. "I mean, Jukin left you for dead on a pirate ship, not to mention murdered Tauron. So why not just give him your inheritance too?"

She watched the ice shift in the glass as it melted a little more and wished Sage would just go away. Instead, she answered, "It's complicated."

"It's really not."

"Do you know why Jukin decided to become a police officer?" she asked. "It was because our father decided to take me as his assistant, and not Jukin." She pushed her drink forward, the ice clinking against the glass. "It didn't matter to Sostas that I was just a kid at the time and Jukin was begging him to take him instead. I was the one who fit the bill, and so I was the one..." She tapped her fingernails on the glass. "And Jukin's just been taking it out on everyone else ever since."

Sage stared at her as if she had two heads. "You think you're responsible for everything Jukin's ever done?"

Lyssa's eyes widened and she realized she'd overshared. Why did she ever think drinking was a good idea? She clenched her jaw to prevent herself from saying anything else.

Sage blew air out between his lips and sat back in the chair. "God in Leveman's, Lyss, you are even more of a mess than I thought."

"Thanks for the news flash." She cracked a smile and picked up the glass, nodding to the bartender for another one.

"C'mon," Sage said, nudging her. "Don't just sit here and get drunk. You're better than that."

"Why? I'm not worth anything."

"Your *bounty* isn't worth anything." Sage nudged her harder. "You, on the other hand, are worth at least a few hundred credits."

She snorted. "You're funny, Teon."

"Come on, where's that fire? Where's that boastful, 'I'm a damned good bounty hunter'?"

"Gone with my bounty." The bartender replaced her drink and she took another sip. "I've tried everything, Sage. It's…I'm out of options."

"You haven't tried everything."

She looked at him quizzically. "What haven't I tried?"

"I mean…and please don't bite off my head…why don't you let me help you?"

He'd made this offer before when she'd been on probation. He had suggested that she take up residence on his ship, acting as his bounty hunter the way she had been Tauron's. Instead of being a free agent, her own autonomous entity, she'd be known as a part of Sage's crew.

She didn't loathe his crew as much as she used to, but it wasn't about that. To accept this help from Sage meant admitting defeat, taking a step down and walking around D-882 with her tail between her legs.

Which, she reminded herself angrily, she was already pretty pathetic, drunk at a bar. Slowly, she nodded, hating herself and sinking down to her folded arms on the bar.

"So you'll let me help you?" he asked.

"Yes," she murmured.

"And you won't bitch and moan about it?" he said, sounding excited. "And you won't be meaner than usual? And you won't be stubborn and idiotic?"

She started regretting her agreement almost immediately, but she nodded.

"Good. Then you're coming with me to the Pirate Ball."

"What?" She sat up so quickly that she became dizzy.

"And you and I are going to shop you around to one of the other runners, right in front of Dissident." Sage smiled. "Two-for-one deal. They take you—off probation—they get me. Unless Dissident changes his mind."

Her jaw dropped and her mind blanked. Sage was going to leave Dissident's web?

For her?

Without a thought, she flew across the seat into Sage's arms, wrapping him in a fierce hug so forcefully she was sure she'd knock him off the barstool. He laughed as he steadied himself, before returning the embrace, his hands sliding down her back. She pulled back a little bit, unable to breathe and unable to even think.

"So," Sage whispered, his voice shaky. "You should call Lizbeth probably."

She searched his face and shook her head in confusion.

"As you'll need a…dress."

In a flash, Lyssa went from elation and gratitude for Sage's magnanimous effort to horror and disgust. She shoved him away and returned to her seat, growling. "I'm not wearing a dress."

"Kind of non-negotiable," Sage said, having the courtesy to at least sound a bit sorry about it. "Runners said that any, uh, *female companions,*"—he coughed nervously as she glared at him—"must be appropriately dressed or else they won't be let in the door."

She glowered but her fight left her. Considering her options were to suck it up and wear a dress or give up bounty hunting entirely, suddenly being a girl didn't seem so awful.

***

Lizbeth was unsurprisingly happy to help Lyssa get ready for the Pirate Ball. Or rather, she was once she quit screaming in happy laughter at the idea of Lyssa in a dress. Lyssa met her halfway between S-864 and D-882 at the transport station G-249, where she walked off the transporter with four bulging bags of makeup and shoes and a dress bag slung over her shoulder.

"Really?" Lyssa asked.

"Shut up, I only get to do this once," Lizbeth said, as she waddled by towards Lyssa's ship.

Lizbeth wasted no time setting up shop in Lyssa's bathroom, the same way she'd done when they were in the throes of investigation. Lyssa took the opportunity to unzip the dress bag, but all she got was a glimpse of black fabric before when Lizbeth's voice stopped her.

"Not yet!" she barked, holding a brush and tweezers in her hand.

Eyebrows plucked, Lizbeth set to Lyssa's hair next.

"Formal" apparently meant something, and so Lizbeth took great pleasure in spraying a pound of hairspray in Lyssa's hair before carefully curling it and pinning half of it up and spilling the rest over her right shoulder.

"Don't make it too obvious, I still need to look like Razia," she said as Lizbeth swiveled the curling iron around another lock of hair and letting it drop onto her bare shoulder.

"Yeah, yeah, yeah." Lizbeth pinned back the lock she'd just curled. "Sage says you were a bit down in the dumps. Everything okay?"

"I saw Jukin again," she whispered.

"After the trial?"

Lyssa nodded. "He told me that he was involved and wondered why I didn't sell him out."

"Hm," Lizbeth said, pressing down on the mound of hair at the base of Lyssa's head. "Do you hate him at all?"

"No."

"Really? After all he's done to you, you don't even hate him...a little bit?"

"It's not his fault he's like that."

"Yeah, and that's what abusers say about..." Lizbeth finished that statement under her breath. She returned to her shelf of make-up and pulled out a pad of powder. "So, Sage finally got you to go out with him."

"I'm sorry, wh—" Lizbeth grabbed Lyssa's cheek and began brushing powder onto it.

"I'm kidding." Lizbeth smiled meanly. "But really, first he jumps out of a ship for you, and now he's giving up his pirate career for you?"

"He's not giving up anything," Lyssa said. "I mean...not really."

"He's willing to leave Dissident's web for you," Lizbeth pulled out a pen and instructed Lyssa to close her eyes. As the pen glided over the base of her eyelid, Lizbeth continued talking, "I mean, that counts for something, doesn't it?"

"He's my friend," Lyssa said, and the pen glided over her other eye. She tried to open her eyes, but Lizbeth barked at her to keep them closed.

"You and I both know he's not helping you because he's your friend, Lyss."

An uncomfortable feeling settled in the bottom of Lyssa's stomach, the same one that she felt when she talked to Sage about Tauron at Lizbeth's parents' house—a mixture of nerves and something else that she didn't want to think about.

"Whatever," Lyssa snapped. "The point is, he's doing it."

"Mmm," Lizbeth said, brushing over Lyssa's eyes. "He is indeed."

"Stop it."

"No."

"Seriously," Lyssa opened her eyes and looked up at Lizbeth, "stop it."

"Fine," Lizbeth said. "Okay, get naked."

Lyssa shook her head, wondering if she'd misheard her friend. "What?"

"I need to help you put it on," Lizbeth said, holding up the dress.

"I think I can put on a dress."

"Are you sure? You're a bit rusty, I hear."

"Get sucked."

"C'mon, don't make me *make you* get naked. Make sure you lose that sports bra, too."

Undressing and covering her chest, Lyssa stepped out of the bathroom where Lizbeth was gingerly holding a piece of black fabric.

"Now this cost me a lot of money so if you ruin it, I will murder you. Understood?"

"Yeah, yeah," Lyssa said, watching the black silky fabric climb up her arm and over her shoulder. She was pleased to see it came all the way to her collarbones, covering her completely. Her reflection drew her attention, and she nearly fell over at the stranger staring back at her.

Red lips, pale skin, dark eyes, she looked like herself but shinier, more polished. The black silk overlaid with black lace was at least the right color, but the way it clung to her curves and her skin was both exciting and alarming. The bottom pooled around her feet. The sleeves extended down to her wrists, and she was thankful that at least she was covered. Lizbeth soon helped her into a pair of sky-high heels that she could barely walk in.

"Okay, zip it up," she said to Lizbeth, who was still on the ground fiddling with the shoes.

That's when she felt Lizbeth apply tape to the sides of her back and press the fabric in.

"What are you doing?" Lyssa said, throwing a look over her shoulder. "Doesn't it zip?"

"Nope." Lizbeth seemed to be enjoying this.

Lyssa spun around and looked in the mirror. Her back was completely bare, the fabric encircling her shoulders and the double-sided tape were the only thing keeping the dress from falling down.

She turned, panicked, to Lizbeth who seemed proud of her handiwork.

"I can't wear this!"

"Well, you are, and you'll shut up about it," Lizbeth said with a grin. "Because you look gorgeous."

"You know how awful they were when I wore that miniskirt, and this is ten times worse!" Lyssa's voice was bordering on a whine. "They don't respect me now, please don't make me do this."

"If they don't respect you now, what harm will a dress cause?"

Lyssa could only whimper helplessly.

"You know how I dress, right?" Lizbeth asked. "And look at me. I'm leading a multi-agency investigation."

"It's different."

"Stop making excuses for people treating you like shit. *Demand* respect and you'll get it."

"I've been demanding—"

"No, you've been asking. You let Dissident put you back on probation."

"Dissident—"

"Didn't you tell me once that you threatened to beat the shit out of him if he put you back on?"

"Yeah but—"

"So why haven't you beat the shit out of him yet?"

"*Because I deserved to go back on probation!*" Lyssa barked, the words coming from somewhere deep within her.

"And why do you feel that is, my love?" Lizbeth adjusted the curls on Lyssa's shoulder. To Lyssa's stunned expression, Lizbeth simply patted her on the cheek. "It's probably the same reason why you can't hate the man who killed your pirate mentor, stole your inheritance, and doesn't even have the decency to recognize you. You should do some thinking on that." She paused gleefully. "After, of course, you have your date with Sage."

"*It's not a date.*"

***

Sage was coming to retrieve Lyssa from the transport station, and in a bit of spaceship round-robin, Lizbeth was to take Lyssa's ship back to the Academy before hopping a transport back to S-864. Lizbeth said it was because they wanted to save Lyssa the credits of parking her ship for a day, but Lyssa was sure it was another attempt to keep her from running away.

As if she could run away in these heels. She needed to lean on Lizbeth to even make it out of her bedroom.

"How do you walk in these things?" Lyssa grunted, nearly rolling her ankle.

"Practice makes perfect," Lizbeth said. "Quit bitching. You'll ruin your makeup."

Grumbling, Lyssa quieted her complaints to focus on the task of putting one foot in front of the other. Slowly, painfully, they made it to the ramp of her ship.

"Wow," Sage's voice echoed.

She glanced up, doing a small double take. Sage stood at the foot of her ramp, or at least, she assumed it was him. The man in front of her was no pirate. Breathtakingly handsome in his tuxedo, Sage had his normally loose and wild hair gelled and combed neatly back. He was watching her with the same sort of amazed appraisal before rushing up to help walk her down.

"Wow," he repeated with a small laugh. "Just…wow."

"Right?" Lizbeth said proudly.

An uncomfortable feeling settled in Lyssa's stomach at their attention. "Stop it, both of you."

Lizbeth stepped away from Lyssa, who wobbled on her heels until Sage took her other arm. "You okay?" he asked.

"I hate these shoes," Lyssa seethed to Lizbeth.

"You'll survive." Lizbeth turned to Sage with a stern expression. "Have her home before curfew, young man."

"Thanks, Liz," Sage said with a wave. Lyssa felt the palm of his hand on her bare back and she snapped upright when the skin connected. Sage retracted his hand as if it were on fire.

"Sorry," he said, his face growing red. "I…whoa…" He stared at her bare back, and she watched his pupils dance up and down the length of her bare skin. Lizbeth's voice was in the back of her mind talking about friendships and Sage, and Lyssa screamed internally to drown it out.

"Let's go," she huffed.

Sage looked forward, his cheeks still tinted pink as he tried to force the smile off of his face and failing miserably.

"What's wrong?"

"Nothing," he said, with a small cough. "You just look… really pretty."

She squirmed and folded her arms over her chest, already regretting this stupid decision, especially when she heard the loud whooping of the crew when she walked onto Sage's ship. They wore tuxedos as well, even the meatheads, who looked like they had retrieved theirs from a thrift store.

"I'm sorry, Sage, I thought you were going to pick up Razia," Ganon cackled. He also looked devilishly handsome in his tailored suit. "Seems like you picked up a lady instead."

In a quickness surprising even herself, Lyssa grabbed Ganon's arm and twisted it behind his back. "Not. Another. Word."

"Nope," Ganon whimpered under her grip. "You got the right girl…"

"Lyss, let him go," Sage said, his hand coming to her bare back again. The feeling was enough to shock her into letting Ganon go. Sage opened and closed his hand in front of him, stammering about needing to see to the ship's departure and bolted out up the back stairs.

"Man, I hope they let you back in the web," Ganon said, massaging his shoulder. "I'd hate to have to live with this will-they, won't-they shit every day…"

# CHAPTER TEN

She had never actually been able to dock her ship within the city of D-882 as either Lyssa or Razia, and she had to admit that it was a lot easier to step into a lift and step out into where she was going. Especially wearing four-inch heels that felt like walking on knives.

She couldn't walk more than a few steps without rolling her ankles, so she held onto Sage's arm as a less-embarrassing alternative to falling on her face. He took care to walk slowly beside her, letting the crew bound off ahead of them in their damned flat shoes.

"I hate Lizbeth," she muttered as she nearly fell again.

"You've mentioned that a few times," Sage replied. "We're almost there."

She bobbled again, and Sage simply tightened his arm while she righted herself. He wore a smile that seemed comprised of infinite patience.

The party was on the renovated sixth floor of the Eamon's building, and when the lift doors opened, Razia's mouth fell open. Downstairs in the grungy pirate bar, the tables and chairs were cheap and dirty. But the room before them sparkled and gleamed with prestige, so much so that even Mrs. Dr. Sostas Peate might not find fault with it.

She drew her eyes from the ceiling adorned with brand new lights to the less-amusing sight of pirates in tuxedos being frisked by men twice their size. At the front of the entryway, a stuffy-looking man stood at a table checking C-cards. Two more giant men stood at the ready in case he should discover a pirate not on the approved list.

Sage guided her forward to the first set of brutes, a curious look on his face. "What's this?"

"Inspection for weapons." The man towered over even Sage, and was thicker than a tree.

"Since when do we have weapons?" Razia asked Sage who shrugged as he let go of her arm to remove his jacket for inspection.

"I'll take her for inspection." VJ, the normal bartender at Eamon's whom Razia regularly threatened, walked forward with a salacious grin on his face.

"Really?" Razia snapped, motioning to her skin-tight dress. The only thing she could see to hide was her mini-computer, strapped uncomfortably to her inner thigh. "Where in Leveman's am I going to hide weapons?"

VJ grinned. "I'm going to enjoy finding out."

She groaned in disgust and held out her arms as he grinned and stepped behind her almost too close for comfort.

"Mind the dress, will you?"

"Don't worry, baby, I'll be gentle," he cooed, sliding his hands down her arms, then down her side. When his fingers brushed against her braless chest, she elbowed him hard in the ribs.

He coughed amusedly and replied in her ear, "That's fine. I'm more of a butt man anyway." His hands floated down her hips, taking their time over her rear, and she squeezed her legs together lest he get any ideas. When he reached her feet, he stood up happily.

"Did you enjoy that?" Razia asked with ice on her tongue.

"I did, actually—"

She grabbed him by the shirt and pulled him in close. "The next time I see you, I'm going to cut off your dick," she whispered before shoving him away and rejoining Sage.

"What was that about?" Sage asked, sliding his jacket over his shoulders again.

She glared at him, and he nodded in understanding, threading his arm through hers for support. They next had to pass two bouncers and a stuffy looking man checking a list of names.

He took one look at Razia and his eyes narrowed. "You *are not* supposed to be here!"

"She's with me," Sage replied easily and gave her a small wink. "I'm allowed to bring a date, aren't I?"

She heard a derisive snort behind her. "Was only a matter

of time before you started sleeping your way to the top."

Razia flushed bright red and turned to see Relleck being patted down behind her. He had a sneer of disgust on his face, especially when Sage's hand rested on the bare small of her back. This time, he did not pull away.

"Let it go, remember why you're here," Sage muttered to her, tossing Relleck a look. "He just wishes he could sleep with you."

"This was a bad idea," she murmured to herself. It was her worst fear realized. Everyone now thought she was simply Sage Teon's bimbo.

"This is not a bad idea," Sage replied before turning to the guard. "Can we pass already?"

"Fine," the guard said, motioning them forward. "You and your crew and your...date are to be seated at table five. Dal will show you to your seat."

Razia did a double take. It was Dal Jamus, the very first bounty she'd taken down after she was off probation the first time. He didn't seem to recognize her, or if he did, he wasn't acknowledging her, as he led them into the room.

"What?" Sage asked.

"Hard to believe I captured him," she said quietly, so Jamus wouldn't hear. "He's humungous."

"You think you could take him down wearing that dress?" Sage teased.

Razia thought about hanging upside-down in her dress and shuddered. "I would prefer to not do anything athletic until I can put a bra back on."

"Wait you aren't wearing a bra?" Sage whistled. "Wow."

Razia wasn't sure if he was commenting on her bralessness or the state of the room. Insurgent had spared no expense in the remodel of this room. Gone were the multiple rooms of dancers, the dull thud of the terrible music, the dim lights. Instead, swaths of shimmering gold draperies hung from newly installed ivory columns. Light, classical music wafted over the quiet conversation of tuxedo-wearing pirates, none of whom she recognized without a few moments of staring at them. Everyone was seated around circular tables covered in white linens and gold silverware.

"This is...pretty impressive," she said, as a waiter strolled by with crystal champagne glasses sparkling delicately.

"Harms was telling me that the runners paid obscene amounts of money to Insurgent for this," Sage said.

"How much of that went to this, and how much went to Insurgent?" Razia asked with a grin.

Sage shared her smile, and her stomach jumped. "I'd say about fifty-fifty."

They arrived at their table, and Razia sat down, thankful to be off her feet again. Sage took the seat next to her and the rest of his crew filled the rest of the table. She rotated in her chair and scanned the room in earnest, checking every face against her memory bank of pirates, marking off who was a top pirate and who—

"Enough," Sage said, interrupting her thoughts. He was pouring champagne into her glass. "Can't you take a break for one night?" He left his glass empty but poured for the rest of the crew.

"I'm looking for the runners," Lyssa said, finally spotting

them at the other end of the room. Even they looked moderately better, although Contestant had taken it an extra step by wearing a vivid purple suit and a matching hat with a giant feather that extended behind him. She narrowed her eyes and turned back around to Sage. "Okay, let's go talk to them—"

"We will, we will," Sage said, gently turning her in her seat to face the front, "but later."

"Later?" she gasped. "Later, I want to get out of here, I need to get back to work—"

"Every single person that you would even consider hunting is sitting in this room," Sage reminded her. "And you aren't going to get the runners to agree to anything while they're sober."

She opened her mouth and then closed it again; he did have a point.

"So, relax. You look gorgeous and literally everyone is looking at you."

She jumped a little bit and became aware of the rest of the room. Indeed, she spotted Max Fried at the next table over, giving her an approving glance. Costa Enoch was next to him, nodding approvingly. On the other side, some of Insurgent's pirates were also talking and pointing at her.

"They're probably talking about how I'm here with you and I look idiotic," she said, swiping the glass of champagne and drinking it. The bubbles tingled as they went down, and she picked up the menu to hide her embarrassment. Again, she was struck with the expense and effort that went into planning this celebration. A five-course meal was on the menu, with only the finest ingredients and a few creatures that Razia was sure were on the Planetary and System Science Academy's list of protected species.

Sage peered over her shoulder to read off the meal order. "This is the most ridiculous thing I've ever seen," he said to Ganon who shook his head. Sage sat back and threw his arm over the back of Razia's chair. "All these pirates, sitting here like they're some kind of fine royalty. Half of these guys are gonna go plow some prostitute tonight."

"I give it one hour before this turns into a total shit-show," Ganon said, raising his glass at Sage. "Fifty credits."

Sage looked to be considering that bet. "Hour and a half and a hundred."

"Forty-five minutes," Sobal piped up from across the table. "And—"

"No, see, this is where you need to learn, kid," Ganon said, helping himself to more champagne. "All the rabble-rousers aren't here yet. They gotta get here and get plastered before things really go to shit."

"Relleck's here," Sage said, nodding to the table on the other side of the room where Relleck glowered angrily. "Who for some reason looks like he wants to kill me…"

Razia couldn't stop a wince before it crossed her face, and both Ganon and Sage noticed it.

"Ooooh," Ganon cooed, "did something happen? Twenty credits says something happened."

"No!" Razia insisted, hoping that Lizbeth's make-up was enough to cover the blush.

"Lyss, did something happen?" Sage said, suddenly

sounding concerned. "Did he try—"

"Leveman's no," Razia shook her head. She lowered her voice and gave Ganon a mind-your-own-business glare. "I… guess I was…seeing him for a while."

"*What?*" Sage's cry of surprise echoed clear across the room and Razia hissed at him to quiet down. Sage, however, was anything but calm. "*Did you sleep with him?*"

"Who in Leveman's are you, Lizbeth?" Razia barked but she couldn't escape Sage's piercing glare. With a heaving sigh, she shook her head. "No. We just…made out a bit. A couple of times."

"How many times?" Sage pressed.

"As many times as it's none of your damned business. Why are you so interested?"

Sage was locked in a battle of across-the-room glares with Relleck. "Are you still seeing him?"

"No," she said darkly, following his gaze and narrowing her eyes. "Apparently when I'm on probation, I'm no longer attractive to him."

Sage's face softened a little before he tossed one final dirty look and rude gesture to Relleck, who returned it with gusto. "You're *always* attractive."

Razia picked up her champagne again and downed it, hoping the bubbles would quickly ease her embarrassment. "Like I said, it wasn't anything…real."

"Good." Sage smiled and adjusted his arm over the back of her chair.

Appetizers arrived, cutting off the awkward moment and conversation, and soon after soup arrived. But two glasses of champagne had loosened the tension in Razia's shoulders considerably, and she actually began to enjoy the conversation with the guys at the table.

Sage, in particular, made an art out of poking fun at the members of his crew who had been downing champagne as fast as it was poured. Razia, not eager to get completely toasted, was still halfway through her third glass while Sage's remained empty.

By the time dessert rolled around, Ganon's voice could be heard from the entire room.

"So I'm in the room with this girl, and she won't suck my dick!" Ganon bellowed. "I said, 'Look sweetie, I did my part, and you gotta do yours.' She won't do it, so I says, 'Yeah, it's probably for the best, cause it's a *choking hazard*!" The drunks at the table roared while Sage simply lifted his eyebrows in patient amusement.

Razia took a dainty sip of her water. "Isn't that the warning they put on small toys?"

A chorus of "*Ohs"* boomed from their table, and from a couple nearby groups that had heard the exchange. Ganon stood and bowed to Razia before guffawing loudly as he plopped down and nearly fell out of his chair.

"I like you," Ganon said. "I retract what I said before. You're welcome on the ship any time."

"That's a big deal," Sage explained solemnly to Razia, who laughed. "Ganon's drunken approval is hard won."

"I can tell," Razia said, nodding to where he was leaning over to the next table and making friends.

"Want another one?" Sage asked, looking to Razia's glass.

"Nah." She looked over at the runners' table. "Think it's time yet?"

He looked over to Ganon and smirked. "Yeah, because pretty soon, I'm going to be doing toilet duty with this one." He shook his head. "And yet tomorrow night, he'll be two shots in before dinner."

Sage helped Razia to her feet, and although the champagne blurred her brain slightly, her feet still stung with every step. She adjusted her dress and steeled herself. "Let's do this."

Sage offered her his arm, but she ignored it, preferring to walk on her own two feet. She was so focused on not tripping that she found herself in front of the runners' table before she knew it.

When Dissident noticed her standing there, he shrank down in his seat, looking visibly annoyed that she was even there. The other runners, however, seemed amused.

"Sage Teon!" Protestor chirped, clapping his hands together. "Did you bring us a present?"

The other runners began to chuckle and Razia's heartbeat quickened with worry. Glancing over at Sage, she saw he was relaxed and jovial, and it put her at ease a little.

"I have a proposition for you all," Sage said. "It seems that I'm in the market for a new runner."

Dissident choked on the chocolate pudding he was shoveling into his mouth, and the other runners suddenly looked interested. Sage was considered Tauron's protégé (Razia shut down her burgeoning feelings of jealousy), and any runner that counted him in their web had bragging rights. At least, that's how Dissident always played it.

"Sage, my boy," Dissident coughed, downing more of his champagne. "What's this all about? I've excused your dues for a year and—"

Razia wasn't sure where to direct her glare. *Her* dues were nearly the cost of a planet excavation.

"Yes, but you haven't done the one thing I've asked of you," Sage said, glancing at Razia. "Take her off probation or I'm going to another web."

"I'll take you, Sage!" Contestant cheered. "Relleck has been getting on my last nerve lately. It'll be nice to have such a—"

"But you have to take her too," Sage said, cutting him off. "Off probation."

Silence descended on the table, more from shock than from consideration, and Razia began to panic. She glanced at Sage again, and he still seemed unaffected.

"She has captured nearly half of your top pirates, and she's got knowledge of Dissident's pirates to be able to pick them off without any problem. You know that she's tenacious. You know she's not going to stop until she finds the bounty. She's found some of the least findable pirates in the universe, including your *son*." Sage pointedly glared at Insurgent, who ducked lower in his chair. "So how's about it?"

"Sage, she's..." Contestant began. "I mean, look at her. If you were offering her for a night or two, I'd say yes."

Her mouth fell open and beside her, Sage grew red with anger.

"Leveman's, Contestant, have some damned decency," he growled. "She's standing right here."

"I wouldn't say no to a night either," Insurgent drawled and shared a cackle with protestor. "Perhaps if she lost the scowl and the chip on her shoulder."

"And that dress," Protestor chirped.

"You are disgusting," Sage said.

Razia opened her mouth to speak, to fire off some witty comment or acerbic barb to put them in their places, but her mind drew a blank. She stood there in this ridiculous dress, in these ridiculous shoes, before with the four men with the power to give her what she wanted. And they were laughing at her.

She spun on her heel and rushed away. She needed to get fresh air, she needed to get out of this room where the humiliation and the embarrassment were choking her. Spying an open balcony, she disappeared through the curtains, not taking a breath until her hands landed on the cold stone overlooking the lower buildings and the rest of the dark pirate city.

"Lyssa!" Sage had followed her, and sounded winded. "What in Leveman's was that?"

She said nothing, looking out into the quiet city.

"Come on." Sage joined her on the railing, much as she'd joined him at Lizbeth's parents' house. "Let's go back in there and—"

"You heard them, Sage," she whispered. "This was never going to work. Nothing…nothing's going to work. Ever."

"What is with you lately?" Sage asked. "You used to laugh

at this shit and now it's like..." He looked back to the room. "You should have mopped the floor with those idiots."

She closed her eyes and rubbed her face, feeling make-up under her fingertips. She wanted to rip off her skin and throw it off the balcony.

"Lyssa, talk to me. What's bothering you?"

"I just..." She had the truth on the tip of her tongue but couldn't force it out. Not in front of Sage. "This was a mistake. A terrible, stupid, moronic—"

"Standing up for yourself and what is right is a mistake?" Sage grabbed her by the shoulders and turned her to look at him. "Not taking that bullshit they dish out is a mistake?"

She remembered Lizbeth's words. But how was she to demand respect from someone who didn't even treat her like a human being?

For so long, she had felt that being a bounty hunter was her calling, but she had tried everything she could think of to make headway and she'd failed. Heelin had said this was what she was passionate about, what she'd been doing since she was a kid. But then again, it was only chance that she had even met Tauron. Perhaps she'd been seeing something that wasn't even there.

"Do you think this is what I'm supposed to be doing?" she asked quietly.

Sage turned to look at her like she had two heads. "What kind of a dumbass question is that, Lyssa?"

She shrugged. "Why do I even want to be a bounty hunter in the first place? Nobody else wants me here." She closed her eyes, hoping to keep her emotions inside. "Even

Tauron didn't think I could do this."

Sage's hands covered hers, and when she opened her eyes, he was staring into them. "Tauron always thought you could do this."

"How many times did he drag me back to the Academy? He was happier when I left. I should've never come back."

"At first, sure."

"You said it took him a while to let me stay on his ship."

"Oh, come on, I was just being...stupid."

"No you weren't. You were being honest. And I should have been more perceptive." She looked down at the street some six stories below. "All of my success has been nothing but dumb luck. The only reason I became a bounty hunter in the first place was because Tauron chose me instead of my brother Heelin."

"That is absolutely not true. Tauron wouldn't have let you hang around if you weren't useful, trust me. Didn't he give you a pirate log-on? Didn't he let you hunt all of his bounties?"

"Yeah, I'd hunt them and he'd make me sit on the ship while he captured them," Razia said, looking at her hands, still covered in Sage's. Hers were tiny in comparison.

"Because..." Sage breathed out through his lips. "Because he was afraid someone was going to...if you got knocked out...and..." He trailed off, disgusted at the very idea. "But he never doubted you." He half-smiled. "Didn't you tell me that? When you care about someone, you protect them?"

His words rang hollow for her. "I wish I could believe you."

"If he didn't believe in you, then why did he put that bounty on you?"

She snorted. "All five hundred credits of it..."

Sage dropped her hands and turned to lean over the balcony. "That's all he had left in the one account that hadn't been frozen," he replied, his voice strained. "The ship was surrounded and there was no way...it was one of the last things he did before...well..."

A chill traveled down her spine and spread across her body. The particulars of how her bounty came to appear on her account, she'd never asked about.

"And yeah, it took Tauron a while to realize the kind of person that you are, what you're capable of," Sage said. "But once he did, he believed in you, and so do I."

She glanced up at him, wondering why it meant so much to her that Sage believed in her.

He looked back into the room and shook his head. "And they'll figure out out one day."

"One day." She laughed. "One day is what I've been planning on forever. And right now, to*day* sucks."

"Well to*night*, you are here at the Pirate Ball with me," Sage said, reaching up to tuck a wayward strand of hair back into place. "And you're going to march back in there and prove to them that you're every bit as amazing as you are. And if I know you, and I do, you won't be down for long. You always figure something out."

"Do you think Vel would let me kidnap him again?" she asked, finally able to crack a smile.

"There's my girl," he said, his hand still hovering on her

cheek. Suddenly, everything in her body began to ring like alarm bells. He watched her with that strange expression, the one that made her insides burn like molten lava. Breathing was now difficult, and even more so when Sage seemed to be inching closer.

*Bam!*

They sprung apart and she covered her heart to keep it from flying out of her chest. But, the noise continued from inside the room, and took precedence over whatever awkward thing had just happened between them.

"What in—" Sage was able to see clearer into the room than she was, and whatever he saw scared him. He yanked Razia into the safety of the darkness.

"What's going on?" Razia asked and then a familiar voice floated out the balcony.

"Round them up. Handcuffs on all of them. No, they're drunk, won't be too much trouble."

Jukin.

# CHAPTER ELEVEN

Jukin was there. At the Pirate Ball. Where most, if not all, of the universe's most wanted pirates had been drinking heavily for the past two hours.

"Fan out, surround them! I want handcuffs on everyone in the next five minutes or it's your ass."

Razia's heart stopped in her chest as reality snapped into focus.

This was bad. Very, *very* bad.

"Sage," she whispered, his body still pressed against hers protectively. "Sage, we need to get out of here."

"My guys are still in there." He sounded far away, his eyes glued on the bright room. When he moved to leave her and walk back into the room, Razia grabbed him by the wrist and yanked him back to her.

"What are you doing? You can't go in there, they'll arrest you!"

He stopped tugging on her hand. "Let me go. I have to get them out of there."

"Sage, there's fifty officers in there," Razia said, squeezing on his wrist tighter and digging in her heels. "You can't possibly—"

"So what, you want me to just leave them in there? Leave them to *Jukin*?"

"Sage, we can't even…we'll figure something out." She tugged on him again, praying that he would see reason. Visions of Sage on the dais at Leveman's Vortex swam in her head.

"We will get them out," Razia said, though she had absolutely no idea how or why or what. "Please. We have to go now, before they come looking out here."

He looked torn between his crew and leaving, and she prayed to the Great Creator that he would see reason. The seconds passed and he wasn't moving to safety, and she began to panic.

"Sage, please. I can't…I can't lose you." His face shifted like he suddenly heard her. "Please."

He reached a hand to her cheek, gently stroking it. "You won't lose me, I promise. But, Lyss…"

"We'll get them out, but we can't if we're—"

"I know." He took one long lingering look into the room, his thumb still rubbing her skin. Conboy Conrad yelped in pain when one of the officers threw him to the ground to handcuff him.

Then without another word, Sage stalked over to the edge of the balcony and leaned over, glancing around. He waved her over and she joined him, her eyes glazing over when she realized they were six stories off the ground.

"There's a balcony down there," Sage said, swinging his legs over the edge of the railing. Before she could respond, he slid off and landed gracefully on the balcony below.

"Sage..." she said, glancing behind her. The Special Forces were still busy with the pirates in the room, but soon they'd come searching outside.

"Lyss," Sage called up to her, "you can do this."

He wasn't that far away, his arms outstretched to catch her. But she envisioned herself slipping out of his grip, missing the balcony entirely. Her palms began to sweat against the stone and she glanced behind her again.

"Lyss!" Sage hissed. "It's okay, you can do this." He shrugged off his suit jacket and held his arms up towards her. "I'll catch you, c'mon!"

She took a shaky breath and hopped on the edge of the balcony, kicking her legs over. She tried to ignore how far the ground was below, but she couldn't tear her eyes away.

"*Lyss!*" Sage's voice shot upwards at her.

Squeezing her eyes together, she pushed herself off the edge and clenched her jaw together so she wouldn't scream. But as soon as she let go, she was in his arms, cradled against his chest. She opened her eyes as he placed her on her feet and cupped her cheek.

"You okay?" he whispered, tilting her head up to look at

him.

"Yeah," she said with a curt nod.

"I heard a noise out here!"

Before Razia could react, Sage yanked her against the wall, out of sight of the balcony above. Razia was sure that her heart was going to give away their location as loud as it was pounding.

"I'm just checking out here, give me a second." Opli was on the balcony. She heard his polished boots clack against the stone, coming to a halt at the edge of the balcony. Razia panicked, wondering if she and Sage had left a sign that they had been out there.

"Sir, did you find anything?" Razia didn't know whom that voice belonged to.

"They aren't here."

Razia exchanged a wide-eyed stare with Sage. He shook his head and slipped his fingers through hers. The small gesture slowed her heartbeat somewhat.

"Are you sure they came?"

"His crew is in there, and he never goes anywhere without them," Opli said.

Razia tightened her grip around Sage's fingers, needing him to not say or do anything stupid. His face was twisted in anger, but he made no sound.

"Sir, we have all the others."

"Captain Peate specifically asked me to make sure they were arrested," Opli said. "Especially the girl."

"We'll get them."

"*I know we'll get them.* But now I have the unpleasant task of informing Captain Peate that we don't have them *now.*"

Their conversation died down as the two officers disappeared back into the main room. Razia exhaled the breath she'd been holding. She cast a nervous glance at Sage, who was still gnashing his teeth in anger.

"Those bastards," he whispered. "What in Leveman's did we ever do to them?"

She tugged on their still intertwined fingers to get his attention. "We need to get away from here. Go somewhere safe and regroup."

Sage let go of her hand and walked to the edge of the balcony they were on, waving her over. "Look, there's a fire escape on the next level down. We'll be able to dip out into the alley from there and get out of here."

"The building is crawling with U-POL," she replied.

"Then we'll just have to be quick." He took her hand again and pulled her into the dark room attached to the balcony. Boxes of stemware and place settings filled the room, some opened, some not. They slowly crept toward the light on the other side of the room, careful to stay out of sight. Sage stopped just short of the door. He waited a few breaths then poked his head out. He nodded to Razia and tugged her down the hall to the next room over, where they would find the fire escape.

Except the door was locked.

"Sage," Razia said, glancing down both directions of the hallway where they were very obviously in danger of being spotted. The building lift was on the far end of the hall, and she saw the numbers light up as the car moved up and down the building. The car was on the bottom floor, but it was slowly rising up.

"Give me a sec," Sage said, pulling out his mini-computer. He clicked a button on the case, exposing two tiny pins. Yanking them out, he began picking the lock on the door.

"Sage."

"Just one second."

"I don't think we have one second," she said, as the lights on the lift began to creep closer to their floor.

"Just…one…."

"*Sage!*"

"*Second!*" Sage said, swinging the door open and pulling her inside just as the lift doors dinged. They sat pressed on either side of the open door, staring at the whites of each others' eyes in the darkness, afraid to move or make a noise.

"So I says, I can't believe that we've been roped into doing this. But then again, Peate says he's gonna pay us pretty well for it."

"I'm gonna miss that monthly bonus, though."

Razia held her breath as two U-POL officers strolled by. They didn't have the gold marks of the Special Forces, and so they bypassed the open door, too engrossed in conversation to bother to do a good job.

Their voices died down and Sage nodded to her. He rushed to the window and slid it open silently, climbing out into the fire escape. She followed and he helped her climb out, but she nearly fell as her heel caught in the grate.

"Damn it," she hissed, struggling to free it. "Lizbeth is…"

Her eyes widened. "Lizbeth."

She pulled out her mini-computer from her hiding spot between her legs and fired off a message.

*Do not go back to your apartment. Go lay low with your folks for a few weeks. I'll call you later.*

She waited for a moment, barely breathing and praying that Lizbeth wasn't already at her apartment. Something about Opli's threat about Lizbeth not being in the pirate web a few weeks ago made her nervous.

Then, *Copy. Stay safe.*

"What are you doing?" Sage hissed up at her from a landing below. She'd been so focused on Lizbeth that she hadn't even noticed he'd moved.

"Nothing," she whispered, reaching down to unhook her shoes. The balls of her feet ached from wearing the heels all this time, and it felt good to be able to walk normally again. She gathered the heels in her arms and silently followed Sage down the fire escape to the alley behind Eamon's.

Sage took Razia's hand and pulled her toward the end of the alley where they peered out into the street.

"I don't see anyone," Razia whispered, leaning over Sage's shoulder.

"Probably too busy upstairs still." He looked down at her feet, brow furrowed. "What happened to your shoes?"

She lifted the heels in her hand.

"You can't go barefoot," Sage said, turning around. "Get on."

"What?"

"We can go faster if you aren't bitching about your feet

the whole time."

"I'm not—" Her protest died in her throat. She swallowed her pride and wrapped her arms around Sage's neck, hosting herself up. The night air was cold on her back but she was grateful that her dress was flexible enough. His hands slipped under her knees, and she shivered at the intimate touch. Together, they slipped out of the alley keeping to the dark patches between the light posts.

"Where are we going?" she whispered, afraid to speak too loudly.

"Home."

She laid her head against his shoulder, a curious expression crossing her face. Sage's home, she assumed, was his ship, currently sitting at Eamon's docking station, but they were certainly headed away from there. They kept to the shadows, even though they were the only souls on the street. There was no sign that the U-POL had expanded their search from Eamon's.

She closed her eyes; they had been *very* lucky. Had Jukin come just a few minutes before, they would have been in handcuffs with the rest of the pirates.

Although they weren't any safer outside of jail, either. She didn't know for sure what Jukin had planned, but she could make an educated guess. The question was, when the executions would start taking place. And how long did they have to figure out a way to extricate everyone from this quagmire.

Selfishly, she was thankful that Lizbeth was on her way to her parents' house, Vel was safely on a deserted planet, and

Sage was there with her.

But Sage's crew wasn't safe.

She tightened her arms around Sage's neck and leaned her head into his.

He adjusted her on his back, thinking she was falling off. "You okay?"

"Are you?"

He didn't speak for a long time. "No."

She tightened her hold again on him again and they continued to walk in silence. With Sage taking the lead, in addition to the lingering alcohol in her brain, she lost track of where in the city they traveled.

Some time later, Sage stopped abruptly in an alley and put her on her feet. Sage walked over to the fire escape and it clanged—loudly—to the ground.

"Sage!" she hissed, looking around for the U-POL to jump out of the trash bins.

"Relax, we're halfway across town, or were you asleep the whole time?" Sage said, his hands on the ladder. "Let's go."

She glared at him as she climbed up the ladder, wondering where he was taking her. They passed dark windows with Sage giving little care for being quiet. He stopped halfway up the building at a window. Feeling along the edge of the pane, he procured a key, which he used to unlock it. He ducked inside and reached out to help Razia climb in as well.

Her bare feet landed on soft, plush carpet. The room was small with a twin bed in the corner and an open closet with boxes inside. There was something familiar about this place, but she couldn't place her finger on when she'd been there before.

"Where are we?" she asked.

"You don't remember?" Sage asked with a small smile. He didn't move to turn on any lights, opting to move through the darkness. She followed him out into the living room where two couches and a half-eaten bowl of food sat in front of an old television. Wherever they were, it looked like someone was actively living there. For a brief moment, Razia wondered if Sage had a girlfriend and was surprised at the flash of jealousy.

Sage was still wandering through the dark apartment. He went to a closed door on the other side and cracking it open. The bed inside the room was unmade, but empty.

"Well, where is—"

Just as something dark flew by his head, Sage ducked and fell down to the ground.

"*Harm's, what in Leveman's?*" he roared. "It's *us*!"

The figure walked into the dim light, and Razia could barely make out the shape of their informant. He reached to the lamp and turned it on, bathing them in yellow light.

"Great Creator in Leveman's Vortex," Harms whispered, putting his hand over his heart. "Sage, you scared..." He trailed off and did a double take at Razia. His head tilted to the side in amazement as he took in the full scope of her outfit—from the high heels in her hands to the skin-tight black dress to her hair, which felt like it was falling out of its carefully pinned coif. "Razia, you look...gorgeous. But I don't understand. What are you two doing here? Shouldn't you be at the Pirate Ball?"

"Jukin showed up," Sage growled darkly.

"I don't…Jukin?" Harms' eyes widened in shock. "Jukin showed up at the *Pirate Ball*?"

Sage nodded, looking to Razia. "We were lucky. When they arrived, we were out on the balcony at Eamon's and escaped."

"Did he arrest everyone?"

"I think so," Razia whispered, hating the way Sage grimaced when she said it. "Everyone was really drunk and —"

"Jukin took advantage of the situation," Harms finished for her. He shook his head angrily. "I *told* the runners this was a bad idea. You know, we're not as safe as we all thought we were. Tauron thought he was safe, too."

Razia winced, but it went unnoticed.

"I don't know how this could have happened," Sage said. "Isn't that what we pay thousands in pirate dues for every month?"

"Is he taking them to that jail?" Harms asked. Unlike the jail Razia had stayed in when she'd been captured by Loeb, the one on the other side of D-882 was where Tauron had been put to death.

"Probably, but he can't fit everyone in there. It was only built for fifty prisoners," Sage said. "There were nearly a hundred by my count."

"I doubt he's planning to hold many of them long term," Harms said.

Razia covered her face in her hands. This wasn't

happening. She just couldn't believe this was happening. Not again.

"Who do you think…?" Sage whispered.

"The…well, probably the runners, and maybe some of the more notorious pirates," Harms said.

*And their crews*, Razia finished silently. Sobal's face popped into her mind's eye. He was just a kid—Vel's age, in fact. He was probably scared out of his mind. Jukin wouldn't kill him, would he?

"Harms, we have to do something." Sage's voice cracked as he spoke.

"And what do you suggest? Storming the castle?" Harms laughed, but it was tinged with sadness. "Sage, I know those are your guys, but—"

"*They're not my guys, they're my family!*"

Razia jumped, not at the ferocity of his words, but at emotion behind them. Sage's face was wild with fear and more emotions than Razia could read. His hands were balled at his side as he stared at Harms. Razia was suddenly thankful she had managed to pry him away from danger; if she hadn't been there…

"Sage—" Harms tried, but Sage wasn't listening. He let out an angry roar and slammed his fist into a nearby wall, leaving a gaping hole. Without another word, he stormed into the back bedroom, slamming the door so loudly it echoed.

Razia was afraid to move. Sage barked at her all the time, but this was different. Her heart began to hurt for him again as she stared at the closed door. A part of her wanted to go after him, but another part of her was afraid to.

"Give him time," Harms said, breaking the silence.

"I don't think we have time," Razia whispered. "We're… we can't let this happen, Harms."

"Razia, listen to me." Harms walked over to her and took her hand in the same gentle way as when she came to him for pirate information. "This is selfish and completely uncalled for, but…" He struggled to find the words to say. Finally, he settled for, "I'm glad that you two are safe. Please stay here tonight." He motioned to the door. "Sage is already in his room, but—"

"He said this was home," Razia said suddenly, not sure why that stuck with her. "Why?"

"This is where he stayed after Tauron died. I let him crash here from time to time," Harms said with a curious smile. "You don't remember coming here?"

The apartment did seem a little more familiar than before. But as the seconds ticked by, exhaustion quickly overpowered her other thoughts. She sank down onto the couch and put her head in her hands. She still felt the make-up Lizbeth had applied. That whole episode seemed a lifetime ago.

"Here." Harms appeared in front of her with a folded up blanket and pillow. "You can sleep on the couch tonight until we figure out what to do."

"Thanks," she whispered, taking the bedding and holding it tight to her chest.

"And that reminds me," Harms said, walking to the closet next to his front door. "Since I'm sure that you don't want to sleep in that dress…"

He procured a small bag from the closet and tossed it at her. She unzipped it and pulled out a shirt, bra, and other clothes. But the patch on the bag caught her attention; it was the official insignia for the Planetary and System Science Academy.

"You left that the last time you stayed here, and I just kept forgetting to bring it back to you."

Her finger ran over the patch. If Harms had wanted to, he could have given this as a hint to any number of pirates who had been searching for her. But he'd never asked or said anything about it.

"Get some rest, okay?" Harms said.

"Harms?" she whispered. She smiled and clutched the bag to her. "Thanks."

Harms smiled at her as he disappeared into his bedroom, closing the door behind him. Razia clutched her clothes and hurried to the bathroom, needing to get into something that wasn't this infernal dress. Her reflection was as she had expected it to be. Her lipstick had all but rubbed off and her hair was falling down her back. Her dress, surprisingly, still clung to every curve of her body, and the double-sided tape Lizbeth had applied seemed to be stronger than the pull of Leveman's Vortex.

"Ow...owowowowow," she hissed, pulling the dress off. She poked at the red marks on her back in the mirror before giving up and stepping into the shower. She ended up using nearly half of Harms' shampoo to wash the gel and hairspray out. But as the soap bubbles washed down her back, she stopped scrubbing and let the full weight of the night crash on top of her.

This was all her fault.

She desperately wished for an undo button, a way to go back in time to when she sat on that podium in front of all the cameras, to change her answer from, "No one else" to "Jukin Peate." Then he would be the one in jail, and Sage's crew would be sleeping off their hangovers on his ship where they belonged, instead of a in jail cell on the other side of the planet

With a heavy sigh, she turned off the water and stepped out, hoping that maybe this was all a bad dream.

# CHAPTER TWELVE

*"In total, one hundred and three pirates were captured last night in a surprise raid by Captain Jukin Peate's Universal Police Special Forces. They were immediately incarcerated in the Adalhard Memorial Jail on the desert planet D-882."*

Sleep did not come easy to Razia, nor to Sage, who joined her on the couch in the predawn hours of the morning. His face showed no emotion, as if all of his good cheer had been stunned out of him. They turned Harms' television to the news, and right around the time the sun's first light streamed through the windows, the pirate story broke.

*"I commend my Special Forces officers for their diligence and preparation for this monumental task. We believed that we could eradicate piracy, and now, we have eliminated a scourge on the*

*UBU for good."*

Jukin spoke on the steps of the U-POL ivory tower on D-882. Behind him stood a few of his loyal officers, but Razia didn't see Opli. She was waiting for the other half of the story —what Jukin planned to do with the prisoners. She had a pretty good idea, but she still kept a little hope that she would be wrong.

The clip played again a half-hour later, and then on repeat at the top of the hour. Each time, she held her breath, waiting for an update on their fate, and each time, she released it uneasily when her worry went unanswered. She kept glancing at Sage, wondering if he would react. His stoic, distant expression was more unnerving than if he flipped over the coffee table.

Some small part of her wanted to cross the small distance between them, to seek comfort in his nearness. But she remained where she was.

Razia had fallen into a dazed sort of half-sleep. As the sun began filtering through the buildings, Sage nudged her gently. She looked at the screen, where there was an empty podium. She blinked a few times, realizing that she was looking at the front of the Presidential Palace, and then at the text on the screen, *"General State to make statement on mass pirate arrest."*

She sat up, suddenly awake. General State had said that he thought Jukin should have been tried for murder; maybe he was willing to step in and intervene now. Maybe he was trying to persuade Jukin to simply keep the pirates as prisoners, to let the justice system do its job.

Sage still said nothing as he sat arms' length away. The

urge to crawl closer to him welled up again.

Movement on the screen drew her attention. General State walked up to the podium, his metal badges glinting in the afternoon sunlight. It was midday on S-864, and Razia hoped that Lizbeth was already to D-66253. She hadn't heard from the investigator since her one-lined response, so Lyssa fired off another message.

General State adjusted his glasses as she had seen him do in the courtroom a few weeks back. He stopped to glance around at the cameras, as if counting them to himself. Then, after a pause that seemed to Razia to last an eternity, he spoke.

*"Piracy has been a blight on our system of universal government for far too long. I commend Captain Peate for his efforts and congratulate him and his team on a job well done."*

Something cold settled in Razia's stomach.

*"I have ordered all available U-POL forces to converge on D-882. I have given Captain Peate the power to command them as he sees fit. I will not be taking questions."*

He walked away from the podium and Razia felt like someone had kicked her in the gut. General State had seemed so reasonable, a neutral party who tolerated the pirates. He'd known that she'd lied about Jukin's involvement and was curious about it. He'd said that he disagreed with Jukin's methods, his obsession.

She turned back to the screen, where the presenter was showing a chart with State's face.

*"The latest polling has General State at twenty points up to any potential contenders to unseat President Llendo."*

The cold chill in her stomach suddenly turned to fire. When she'd first covered for Jukin, State said that he would have had him tried for the murder of Tauron if it weren't for "the political headwinds." And now, he was refusing to do the right thing because not doing so benefitted him politically.

She'd been completely wrong about General State. He wasn't a man of any backbone; he was simply a politician.

The screen flashed with the "Breaking News" graphic, and Razia closed her eyes, not wanting to see what was about to be announced.

*"The first set of executions will take place in three days. General State has authorized the execution of Lane Podvoisky, known as Dissident, Tomeka Rising, known as Contestant, Victor Femenias, known as Insurgent, and Aldrich Phrase, known as Protestor. Captain Peate said he is in the process of triaging pirates based on their crimes. The most egregious offenders will be executed within the week, with others receiving life sentences."*

Sage made a noise and clenched his jaw.

"So no judge, no jury?" Harms was awake and standing behind them in his sleeping clothes. The presenter continued talking about the plans for the mass execution like it was a simple political tussle. "This is sick. Why isn't there more outrage? Doesn't anybody remember these are people?"

But Razia knew in the grand scheme of the universe, most people didn't care one wit about pirates. They were the scum, the lowest of the low. The runners only received their protections because of the money funneled to the right people. Without that leverage, they and everyone else in jail were powerless to change their fate.

"Lyss."

She looked at Sage, as that was the first word he'd spoken since the night before. She followed his gaze and found herself looking at her own face, next to Sage's, on a wanted poster.

*"Captain Peate has asked for the public's help in finding these two fugitives. He has personally funded a two billion credit reward for anyone who assists in the capture of the bounty hunter named Razia and the pirate Sage Teon."*

"What?" Razia exclaimed, nearly flying off the couch. "He can't put a bounty on us! That's...that's illegal!"

"He's playing our game," Harms said with a grim sort of appreciation. "Money motivates. Now everyone's on his side."

Razia sank back into the couch, her jaw open in shock. Two billion. Where would he get two billion credits to...

Her inheritance. That stupid money was cursed, she decided.

"You two need to get going," Harms said with a new urgency. "They know you're close with me. They might come to find you here."

"Then what?" Razia exclaimed with a nervous look to Sage.

"Disappear to wherever you go to," Harms said. "I don't know where you go, nobody does. Take Sage with you and just...just go, Razia."

It would be so simple to walk away. For the past few weeks, all she could think about was whether it was time to hang up her boots and remain Lyssa Peate forever. And now, the safest thing to do—the easiest thing to do—was to give up on Razia. She and Sage could start fresh and no one would be the wiser.

But she couldn't.

Not when Sage's crew was still in danger, not when there were a hundred and three lives hanging in the balance because *she* had made the wrong decision about Jukin. Not with how she could practically feel Sage's pain from across the room. It was as bad as the night on Joe and Billie's deck…

She blinked. "Didn't you say you had a plan?"

"What?" Harms asked.

"Sage, you said that you had a plan to get Tauron out of that jail."

Sage's face twisted from anguish to confusion. "I…"

"Razia, don't you even think about it," Harms exclaimed. "I talked Sage out of it three years ago because it was idiotic."

"Sage said it would have worked."

"Well, once you make it past the thousands of miles of desert," Harms began, "then you'll have to try not to step on a landmine in the fifteen mile radius surrounding the prison."

"Space jump?" Razia offered.

"The roof is covered in sensors, and, I'd wager at least a patrol of fifty U-POL officers now," Harms said. "Razia, I can appreciate what you're trying to do but, you two just need to accept that this…this has happened."

Razia couldn't accept that. She turned to Sage, "If you could have saved Tauron, would you have done it?"

Sage sighed and nodded. "Of course I would have, but

Lyss...I mean...Harms is right. This...is..." He trailed off, unable to finish the sentence aloud.

"So we'll figure out a way to get into the prison," Razia insisted. "There has to be a way."

"Maybe before, but not now," Harms said. "That bounty pretty much ensures that Jukin's swayed every U-POL officer to his side. The only way you could get onto the prison is if you were invited in, and I daresay that even General State isn't allowed on the planet anymore."

"We could kidnap State, take him hostage and force him," Razia started.

"Lyssa, give it up!" Sage barked, standing up. "I appreciate what you're trying to do, but—"

"Heelin."

The idea came to her like a flash of lightning. Something about him calling her Lyssa sent her mind racing to the other life. She had used Lyssa to get what she wanted before, but calling Jukin as Lyssa and asking him to let her come to the planet was laughable. *Heelin*, on the other hand, would be a willing participant in the charade. If she could just manipulate him the right way.

"Who is Heelin?" Harms asked.

"Sage," Razia grinned, excitement taking hold at the brilliance and riskiness of her instant plan. "If I promise you I can get us in the front door, can you do the rest?"

Harms was still trying to get her to see reason. "Razia, you need to—"

"How solid is your plan?" Sage asked, looking more alert than he had all morning.

"Shaky, but it'll work. We just need to get to the Academy."

"I'm in," Sage said and her heart began to race.

"Sage, you can't be serious," Harms cried. "You're the sane one here!"

Sage ignored Harms as his eyes focused on Razia. "We'll need to get to my ship. I'll need equipment once we're inside the prison."

Harms couldn't believe what he was hearing. "I'm sorry, did you miss the part about the *two billion credit bounty* on your heads? The fact that you two are the most wanted people in the universe?"

"Ooh, who's number one?" Razia asked.

Sage rolled his eyes. "Really?"

*Bam! Bam! Bam!*

Razia nearly jumped out of her skin as all eyes went to the door.

"John Harms? Open up!"

Harms put his finger to his lips and motioned to the second bedroom where they had entered the night before. Razia shook her head violently as Harms moved toward the door.

"Go, I'll be fine," Harms whispered, pushing her. "Please don't get yourselves killed."

"Likewise." Sage nodded to him, reaching out a hand to clasp Harms'. Sage held on for a few extra moments and then let go, his hand coming to rest on Razia's arm. He tugged her towards his bedroom, looking like he'd rather stay there in the room with Harms. Once through the door, Sage closed the door behind them softly and they heard Harms open the door on the other side.

"Yes, how can I help you?"

"We have reason to believe that known fugitives are here."

Opli.

"I'd say you got most of them last night," Harms replied in his kindest voice. "Do you need a cup of coffee? I bet you've been up all night."

"C'mon," Sage whispered in Razia's ear, and they crept across the room to the fire escape. Sage gently opened the window, careful not to make a sound, and slipped out onto the fire escape.

"Shit," Sage mouthed to Razia as he pointed down. She peered down to the alley below and saw two U-POL officers on either side. And while two officers wasn't that big of a deal, two officers with Secure Solution's finest firearms was a different story.

"Sage," she whispered, listening to the conversation in Harms' apartment.

"...they aren't here, I promise you..."

"...still have a warrant to search..."

"We need to make a decision," Razia whispered. Sage grabbed her hand and guided her down the same fire escape they had climbed up the night before. They reached the next landing, and Razia heard Opli's voice through the open window above.

"Why is the window open?"

"This is my smoking room."

"I don't smell any smoke."

"See? It works."

She and Sage flattened themselves against the brick wall and held their breath. Opli's head poked out the window, and Razia was sure he was going to find them, pale and scared against the wall. But he retracted his head back into the room.

She almost sighed in relief, but then:

"Opli to base. Tell all officers that the two fugitives are in the southwest quadrant of the city. I want all resources not assigned to the prison to scramble here ASAP."

"Shit," Sage muttered, his hand still clasping hers. Quietly, they climbed down the fire escape, pausing only momentarily at the last landing before the ground to make sure the two U-POL officers were not looking into the alley. Their attention appeared to be on the street, so Razia and Sage hopped to the ground silently and scurried in-between two giant trash bins.

"Any ideas?" Razia asked, crouching down with Sage against the wall. Sage looked at the officer on the left then the one on the right, and considered. He pressed his finger to his lips and motioned for Razia to stay there. She crouched down, still not sure what he was doing.

He tilted his head up and put his hand to his mouth and called out, "Oy! Come here, I need to take a piss!"

Then he jumped next to Razia, crouching down next to her and holding his breath.

"What'd you say?" The U-POL officer was walking through the alley, right by them, more interested in hollering to his friend on the other side. After he passed them, Sage leapt up and with two quick punches, the officer slumped down.

"*Sage, look out!*"

*Bam!*

Hearing the noise, the other U-POL officer fired at them. Sage ducked and for a brief moment, Razia was terrified he'd been hit. But he flashed a grin at her before taking her hand and yanking her out of the alley.

"They'll be coming out of the woodwork now," Razia muttered, looking all around them.

"There's a lot of city to cover," Sage said, but they ducked into the safety of another alley. A heartbeat later, three U-POL officers ran by, guns drawn. "But they'll be combing the streets." Sage looked up at the sky. "And the rooftops too."

Razia noticed a familiar sight on the corner—a sign for the notoriously broken shuttle system.

"Think they'll go underground?" she asked.

He followed her gaze and furrowed his brow. "Does that thing work?"

"Of course it works," she scoffed, allowing herself to feel jealous that he never had to deal with the horror that was the D-882 shuttle. Then again, if he thought it didn't work, maybe the officers wouldn't be down there checking for them either

"Then let's try it," Sage said, looking up as a U-POL ship flew overhead, "because I am out of ideas."

A hundred feet lay between the safety of the alley and the opening for the shuttle, and if they were seen, then they'd be trapped.

"Ready?" Sage asked, his fingers tightening around hers.

"Let's do it."

They burst from the alley, flying as fast as their feet could carry them across the dusty streets and practically dove into the shuttle station stairwell. Pressed against the wall, they waited for the sound of anyone who had seen them. After an eternity, Razia nodded to Sage, and they continued down to the station.

"Whoa!" Sage's voice echoed down the shuttle station. Razia forgot to mention the long, multi-level escalator that took them far underground. Harms' stop had the deepest station for whatever reason, and it was always a pain in the ass. It boded well for them that it was currently off, although it meant a long, quad-searing trek down the staircase.

"They could have made this shorter," Sage muttered, pausing half-way down the stairs to rub his legs. "You do this all the time?"

"I mean, sometimes it's moving."

They continued down until they reached the station, where Sage took a moment to examine the station with a bit of wonder.

"Is the shuttle running?" he asked, looking at the peeling shuttle map.

"Since the pirate runners pay for it, probably not," she said, hopping over the turnstiles into the dark and empty station itself.

Sage blanched. "Wait, so Dissident pays for this?" He looked around. "No wonder it's a piece of shit."

"Right?" She walked to the edge of the station platform and looked into the tunnel. "If we take this tunnel, we'll have to pass two stations, then transfer to another tunnel and take five stops to get to Eamon's."

"Looks really dark in there, Lyss. You sure they aren't running?"

"C'mon," she said, jumping down onto the tracks and pulling out her mini-computer, facing it down for a little bit of light. Sage followed behind her, his mini-computer joining hers as their footsteps echoed in the near pitch-black darkness.

"Creepy." Sage's voice echoed next to her. She could feel him brush against her arm every few steps.

She couldn't help but tease him. "Afraid of the dark, Teon?"

"Not even a bit." She felt him brush against her again. "Just hope we don't get run over by a shuttle."

"I think we'll hear it before it does. Or see it."

She spotted the first station up ahead and nudged him. "Quiet," she whispered. "Just in case."

But the station was as empty as the first, as was the second and third, where they had to choose between two tunnels at the transfer point. Razia took a few moments to consider the direction they were walking in and chose the one on the left.

"Are you sure?" Sage asked as she hopped back onto the tracks next to him. "We don't have time to be taking a sightseeing tour of D-882's shuttle system."

"Unlike you, I have excellent spatial reasoning."

Even though their conversation was light, Razia was starting to worry about the minutes passing, knowing they had only two days to formulate a plan before Jukin implemented his.

"So where are we in relation to the docking station?" Sage asked as they scurried out of the tunnel and into the station.

"Across the street," Razia replied as they climbed the stairs, turning another corner at a landing. Before she could say another word, Sage's hand flew over her mouth, and he pulled her back sharply against the wall. Lifting his hand, she nodded her understanding at the silence, and peered up the stairs into the street above. No less than fifty U-POL officers milled the street in front of them.

Sage motioned for her to follow and they moved down a distance away from the opening to talk.

"So about this great plan…" Sage said.

"Oh, what, you're going to let a couple of guys scare you off?" Razia asked with a grin. Sage gave her a tired look and she rolled her eyes. "Look, all we need is a diversion. One of us gets them to follow us away from the docking station, the other goes to the ship."

Sage nodded grimly. "The code to open the ship is 54742, and you'll need to use my mini-computer to turn it on, but you can just use autopilot—"

"Hang on, why are you telling me all this?" She put her hands on her hips. "You're going to get the ship, right?"

"No, you are. I'm the distraction."

"No, *I'm* the distraction."

"No way," Sage said firmly. "I am not letting you—"

"You aren't letting me do anything, I'm doing it—"

"This is not the time for you to be stubborn!"

"I'm not being stubborn, I'm being strategic!" she hissed

back. "I'm the faster runner, and I have no idea how to fly your damn huge ship!"

"But…" Sage shook his head violently. "No way, it's too dangerous."

"It's too dangerous for you, too."

"Lyssa, I'm not…" He trailed off. "What if something happens to you?"

"What if something happens to you?"

He clenched his jaw as she waited for his next flimsy excuse. Instead, he yanked her into his arms, squeezing her tightly to him. She breathed him in for a moment, his scent and embrace familiar now. He pulled back to search her face.

"If you get yourself killed, I am going to be so pissed at you," he said.

She cracked a grin. "What else is new?"

"It shouldn't take me that long," Sage said. "How do I find you?"

"I'd say look for the gaggle of U-POL officers chasing the person down the street…"

Sage's face contorted into a tired scowl. "Please don't goad them or taunt them or do anything to make them want to—"

"I won't," she insisted.

Silence fell between them and she suddenly became aware that she was still ensconced in his arms. She noticed his hands resting on her back, the feel of his breath on her face as he watched her, as if he were trying to decide something.

Whatever he was thinking, he decided against it, gently removing his arms from her and turning towards the street again. She shivered a little, surprisingly cold in the dark tunnel. Even though his hands were gone, she still tingled where he had held her.

# CHAPTER THIRTEEN

As she crept up the staircase, Razia thanked herself for the foresight to wear running shoes with her Academy uniform. She wasn't so concerned about the U-POL recognizing the patch, unless they caught her, in which case, she'd have a lot more to worry about.

She paused at the top landing, waiting a few moments for Sage to make his way back to the darkness of the station below. She peered out, scanning the streets and pulling up the map in her mind, trying to come up with a plan to draw them away from there. Most of the officers on the street were the regular U-POL, puffy and out of shape. But she spotted one gold-flecked

She ducked when the one U-POL Special Forces officer

with the giant gun turned to scan in her direction. After a moment, she checked again, and he was peering somewhere else.

A shadow zoomed overhead, and she spotted several small spaceships patrolling the streets from the air. Oblong with two small wings adorned with the U-POL symbol, they seemed only big enough to hold a single officer. Razia didn't fail to notice the giant gun perched on the nose of the ships. These out-of-shape officers wouldn't be able to keep up with her, but the giant ships would overpower her in a minute.

And yet, she looked at their wingspan and guessed they might not be able to make it through the narrower alleyways.

She returned to her internal mapping, remembering that Eamon's was in the south central part of the city. She'd have to run north to give herself plenty of city, if only to avoid getting trapped on the open sands of—

"OI!"

"Damn!" she hissed, having been spotted by a portly officer across the street. A loud crack echoed and two bullet holes appeared next to her head. Without another word, she flew out of the safety of the station and ran down the street.

As more gunfire flew by her, she ducked and increased her speed, adrenaline powering most of her pace. Calculating that most of the officers wouldn't be able to shoot at her and run at the same time, she just needed to get far enough away from them to—

"Hold it!"

She ducked an officer that appeared out of an alley and leaped for her. She didn't look back as his body hit the ground with a loud *thwap*. With a twist on her heel and a hand on the brick corner of the nearby building, she flew into an open alley, pausing only to throw a few giant trash bags behind her to slow down the officers who were still able to keep up.

She laughed to herself as she spotted the few who appeared in the alley moments after she did, and she continued running out of the alley into the open street.

Where she nearly tripped over her own two feet.

There were four U-POL flying ships no larger than the size of Lizbeth's dad's truck hovering in the center of the street, each with their front-mounted guns pointed at her. The glass top opened on one of the ships, and the officer stood, his voice barely audible over the hum of the engines.

"Razia, you are hereby under arrest for—"

She spun on her heel and flew under the four ships before they could change course, bullets piercing the spot where she had just been standing. Predictably, they took a few seconds to re-orient and fly after her. She tossed a look back, gauging their size again, and then dove into another alley. Bullets flew, but the ships couldn't fit.

She saw an open window and took the opportunity, diving into the opening and letting the pane slam down with a loud noise.

She panted for a moment, sliding down against the wall with her hand over her pounding heart, more from fear and adrenaline than exertion. She heard the sound of officers barking in the alleyway, but they left the window alone.

She was in a woman's bathroom (funny she could never

find one of these when she needed one before) in what she could only guess was some bar or cafe near Eamon's. Quietly, she cracked the door and looked out into the dark, open room. Tables were situated around the room with empty chairs placed haphazardly around them, but the room itself was empty of people. She lifted her head up a little more to glance out the giant front windows, spying the growing horde of U-POL officers amassing outside.

She hissed to herself, closing the bathroom door again, pulling out her mini-computer and pressing the power button. When it didn't flash to life, she cursed foully and realized she'd killed the battery using it as a flashlight. She knew she should have replaced the stupid thing.

"Shit," she hissed, leaning her head against the wall. She was counting on using her mini-computer's locator services to help Sage find her.

That is, if he'd even gotten to his ship without being captured.

She pushed that thought out of the way and moved onto her hands and knees to crack open the bathroom door again. Crawling across the floor, she kept out of sight of the large windows and made her way to a backroom door and closed it behind her. Backrooms, she reasoned, might have a back stairwell to an upstairs room or the ceiling.

Popping to her feet, she opened each of the closed closet doors in the room. They only opened to small closets except one that she assumed went out to the back alley that was locked with a deadbolt.

"Shiiiiiiit."

She spun around again, hoping she'd missed a door in her haste. No such luck.

Except when her eyes traveled upward to the ceiling and she spotted the trapdoor.

"*Come out with your hands up*!" The voice came from inside the bar.

Not waiting another second, Razia yanked the cord, not caring that the ladder made a loud crashing sound as it flew down. She scrambled up the steps as fast as her feet could carry her, spilling into a storage room above the bar.

She heard the U-POL officer barge into the backroom, and she glanced about wildly, spotting another fire escape outside a window. She ran to the window, tossing a few boxes towards the open door where the U-POL was climbing up.

"She's in here!"

Razia tossed open the window to the fire escape and hopping out.

"*There she is*!"

"Shit!" Razia hissed but climbed out anyway. The fire escape rattled as she raced up the steps, but fear of being caught overpowered fear of heights. She slid into the window on the top floor, landing in a long, carpeted hallway lined with doors. Apartments, probably, based on the smell of half-cooked food permeating the area.

"*Stop*!"

She spun around, spotting two officers at the other end of the hall. She turned the other way and saw another door. She bolted towards it, hoping that the U-POL wouldn't fire at her and risk hitting a civilian.

She reached the door and kicked it open, revealing a long stairway upwards. The officers barreled towards her, and she flew up the stairs two-by-two, bursting out of the door onto the gravelly roof.

"Well, well, well." Opli and twenty officers had met her there.

She clenched her jaw and swallowed nervously, glancing behind her. The U-POL surrounded her and her only hope was that Sage would be able to find her sooner than later.

She looked to her right and left at the gun-mounted U-POL ships hovering nearby, drowning out nearly every other sound. She wouldn't be able to hear Sage coming until he was right on top of her.

She needed to buy herself as much time as possible, so she chuckled and placed her hands on her hips, trying her damndest to not look as completely scared as she felt.

"You know," she called over the hum of the U-POL ships, "I'd been needing a good run for a while. Thanks for the chase."

Opli's face was awash in a gleeful sort of smugness that put her on edge. Somehow she found him even more reckless than Jukin.

"You always have a line for everything, don't you?" he said, slowly walking towards her as if he had all the time in the world.

Razia couldn't resist a small test. "Familial trait."

Opli's eyes showed no sign of recognition, and she tried to hide a nervous swallow. She thought she heard the rumbling sound of a much larger ship. Opli approached her, surveying her with an appreciative sort of up-and-down.

"And here I'm wondering if I shouldn't just spare us all more of those lines and just kill you myself."

"I can tell you right now that Jukin wouldn't like that at all."

"Indeed not. He's got plans for two extra nooses to go with those damned disgusting pirate runners."

Her heart stopped.

Had they captured Sage?

"Looks like you only have one extra person," she said, hating how nervous her own voice sounded. "You may have to disappoint him."

Opli simply smiled. "I am going to enjoy putting these handcuffs on you." He pulled them from his belt, the metal glinting in the sunlight.

Razia took a step backwards, adding, "Is that your kink? I took you for more of a basic missionary sort of fellow."

As he approached her, the hum that she'd been hearing for the past few minutes grew louder and his face shifted. A shadow fell across the rooftop, and Razia grinned at Opli's apparent concern.

"Sorry, my ride's here."

"W—" Opli gasped. In his momentary distraction, she reared back and punched him in the face, then spun him around and put his body in front of hers, as the U-POL guns aimed at her. But they wouldn't dare shoot at her, not when she had Opli.

"Haven't we been here before?" she chuckled, watching the blowback from Sage's ship send the smaller U-POL ships spiraling away. He turned his engines to point at the rooftop, sending the U-POL onto their backs.

"Go ahead and run away," Opli said. "There is nowhere in this universe we won't find you."

"Oh, I can think of a few places," she said as Sage lowered the hatch on the back of his ship. She surveyed his face and his body, happy to see him without any major injuries. But now she had to figure out how to get from the roof to the ship without either falling into the alley or getting shot.

She edged back towards the edge of the roof, growing more nervous as she realized the distance to the ground.

"*C'mon*!" Sage bellowed to her as the U-POL officers came to their feet.

With a heave, she shoved Opli forward. Spinning on her heel, she took off running on the roof and pushed off, her heart stopping as she cleared the roof and landed on the edge of Sage's extended loading ramp. She barely had a grip before Sage's strong arms latched onto her, pulling her upwards as if she weighed nothing.

Bullets bounced around them, and Sage pulled her closer into the safety of the ship. He stepped back, his hands still on her hips, searching her body for injury.

"I'm fine," she said, but didn't move to remove his hands. "Let's get out of here before—"

"Oh, Razia!" Opli stood on the edge of the roof, still glowing in gleeful smugness. "I'll be sure to say hi to your friend Harms for you!"

The rest of his words faded as Sage closed the hatch.

***

Lyssa lay on Sage's bed, the images of naked women peering down at her with their flirtatious smiles. Sage was still on the bridge, making sure they encountered no trouble while they left the D-882 system, but Lyssa had made it only as far as his bedroom. She needed to curl into a ball under Sage's comforter. Under there, at least, she could pretend everything wasn't happening.

They'd arrested Harms, which she supposed she should have assumed, but hearing the glee in Opli's voice concerned her. They wouldn't push up the executions, would they?

Was Jukin that sadistic?

And even more pressing: could she forgive herself if anything happened to Harms?

"Hey." Sage appeared in the doorway. He looked tired as he plodded towards the bed, kicking off his shoes. Without saying another word, he flopped down on the bed next to her, unleashing a torrent of uncomfortable feelings.

She coughed. "Um, excuse me."

"What?" His words were muffled against the bedsheets. "'s my bed."

"Yeah, but I'm in it right now."

"So?" He turned his face to look at her, and she suddenly noticed the sparkle in his eye. Or more specifically, how it caused her heart to skip a beat. "What's next after we get your ship?"

"Then we head to the Academy to get my brother Heelin," Lyssa replied, looking at the ceiling to avoid him, "and hope that I can convince him to convince Jukin to let him join the U-POL force today."

Sage's eyes flew open and he pressed himself up on the bed. "That's your plan?"

"It's a great plan, thank you very much!"

"We are risking life and limb on the off chance that you can convince your brother, who presumably hates you like the rest of them—"

"Not as much as the rest of them."

"—that he should drop his career—"

"That he hates."

"—and join the U-POL forces?" Sage finished.

Lyssa huffed, looking at the ceiling and realizing that her plan was as stupid as he made it sound. "Well! I didn't hear you coming up with any ideas!"

Sage pinched the bridge of his nose. "And how does your brother joining the U-POL forces get us into the prison?"

She winced. She hadn't fully formulated that part of the plan. "Well, I was gonna ask Jukin nicely to let me drop him off..."

"God in Leveman's, Lyss," Sage sighed and pressed his face back into his pillow.

"I'm working on it!" she huffed. "At least we're off D-882."

"Yeah, you and I always seem to be the only ones who survive your brother's vendettas."

She knew he was speaking generally, but he reminded her of the simple fact that if she'd done the right thing, none of this would be happening.

"Sorry." Sage lifted his head off the bed. "I shouldn't take this out on you."

"I—yeah," she whispered, curling her knees under her and averting her eyes. She could feel Sage's eyes on her, and she desperately needed to change the subject. "So assuming my plan works, how do we break them out?"

Sage turned onto his back and looked at the ceiling as he spoke. "When the prison was built three years ago, it was done in a hurry. They had planned to go back and fix a lot of the vulnerabilities, but never got around to it since there weren't ever any prisoners. And they figured if they did have any, the miles of desert and land mines would be deterrent enough. So within the prison itself, we can cause a lot of confusion pretty easily."

"That's good news, then?"

"Just wait. There are five wings in the prison," Sage said, pulling out his mini-computer. A quick search of his files displayed the blueprints of the prison. "There's one loading dock here at the north end, a wing on the east and west, and two facing southward. Each wing is connected to a main control center at the hub of the wheel. They built it that way to stymie any potential prison riots, but it also cuts off those in the wings from each other. Sobal's got a virus he built for me that we use in jobs sometimes—it reroutes emergency signals. So when the southwest wing hits their emergency signal, the command post thinks it's coming from the east wing. They send their reinforcements there while you take that one, and I'll take the west."

"But how are we going to take the wing with just one person?" Lyssa asked, laying her head on his shoulder as she examined the plans. "I'm good, but I'm not *that* good."

Sage laughed rumbled under her. "Humble at last, are we?"

"Answer the question, ass."

"The virus is customizable, I can set it to do a lot of things —turn off laser sensors, open prison doors, close other ones." He pointed to the door symbol on the blueprint. "These emergency doors are on each of the wings and essentially cut off the wing from the rest of the prison. Once the reinforcements are in the wrong wing of the prison, we'll lock them in there."

"And what about us?"

He pointed to a small box in each wing. "There's emergency generators for the lights, but they won't kick on for about a minute, so that gives our guys time to take down some of them."

"You think they'll move that fast?"

"I think that they'll get the general gist of what's going on."

"After that, then what?"

"You'll have some guys, I'll have some guys, and some of their guards will still be trapped in the east wing. So we take the control center."

"Why don't we just set off the virus and open all the gates?" she asked. "Wouldn't that be smarter?"

"This is all predicated on whether we can do all of this without Jukin finding out." Sage pulled down his mini-computer, typing quickly to display the radar on the planet. Razia guessed there were at least a hundred dots circling the planet. "One distress call and the swarm of U-POL officers descend to quell the violence."

"And you can't cut off that line?"

"The one thing they got right in this place was the failsafe," Sage said. "If you cut it, it'll send a backup emergency signal. And I don't think we have the time for me to try and figure out how to code a counter."

"But even so, what if there are enough officers in the prison to handle a riot?"

"Then we're screwed."

"Right," she said, realizing that his plan was about as harebrained as hers.

"Right," he whispered with the same resignation.

They lay in silence for a moment, and Lyssa had a new thought. "Sage?"

"Hm?"

"If this was your plan three years ago...to get to Tauron...how did you plan to get out of the prison?"

"I didn't expect to make it out."

She half-smiled against his shoulder. "I'm glad Harms stopped you."

He turned to look at her, his face a few inches from hers. She noticed his scent, the shape of his nose, the darker strands mixed in with the lock of golden hair that had fallen on his face. And then she noticed the dark ring that encircled the sea green color of his irises, how his eyes were framed by his dark eyelashes. His pupils danced as he watched her indecisively.

Those alarm bells began to ring again, and she wrenched her face away from his, as nervous and breathless as when she faced Opli and twenty U-POL officers.

"We should start getting ready," she announced, pulling herself out of the bed and racing toward the door as fast as she could.

***

Some time later, Lyssa was waiting down in the bottom of the ship, waiting for Sage to join her. They'd finished packing two black bags of gear (Sage did most of the packing, Lyssa just watched), when he said he needed to run upstairs to get his "disguise."

Lyssa had no idea what that meant until he appeared in the stairwell, wearing a crisp blue button-up shirt and a pair of dark pants, complete with a white lab coat and a pair of smart silver framed glasses. His hair was combed backward, much like at the Pirate Ball, and he wore a small Academy badge at his lapel, which also contained three pens.

"What in Leveman's Vortex are you wearing?" she asked.

"Dr. Alejandro Oriol. Pleased to meet you," he said with a grin. At her dubious expression, he soured. "What? It works for you."

She continued to stare at him.

"I needed an alias!" Sage exclaimed.

"And is that a real badge?" She craned her neck to look closer and spotted the hologram and chip that completed the card which opened doors in the Academy.

"I'm thorough."

"Thorough is one thing, that's...overboard," she said, still peering at the card. "When did you get an Academy alias?"

"I don't know, Lyssa, one of the fifteen times I had to come find you and save your ass. Does it matter?"

"Yes, because it's weird. What do you mean coming to find me? How often are you at the Academy?"

"Instead of worrying about why I have an alias for the Academy, how about you focus on how we're going to get *to* the Academy," Sage said with a hint of a blush on his face.

The subject change was enough, and she grimaced. There was no way they could get Sage's ship to the Academy docks. The only alternative was to dock at a populated station and hope it took the computers a few moments longer to update. Razia decided on the transport station at G-249, as it had one with a non-stop shuttle to the Academy.

She only hoped that they could get onto a shuttle before the U-POL found out Sage's ship had docked here and shut down all transporters leaving the station.

Shouldering the smaller of their two black bags of gear, she listened to the familiar creaking and moaning of the ship as it entered into the station. Sage pulled the other bag onto his shoulder, a grim nervousness etched on his face.

"I hope they're not there waiting for us," he said, his hand on the hatch, ready to release it the moment they landed.

She shifted the bag as the engines rumbled to a stop. "Me too." She jumped when the hydraulics on the ramp creaked to life. Sage joined her and slid his hand into hers, squeezing it gently before releasing it.

The ramp wasn't even halfway lowered before they raced off to hide behind some large boxes that the transporter next to them had unloaded. Not even a second after they crouched down did the lift open and five U-POL officers rushed into the room.

"That was close," Sage whispered and she nodded in agreement.

The transport station on G-249 was one of the largest in the universe, a central location for travelers without ships to converge and transfer between shuttles. This was where she used to sneak onto transporters headed toward D-882 and Tauron when she was at the Academy. It was also where she and Lizbeth found Relleck picking up stolen guns and delivering them to S-864.

The ship docks were on the lowest levels of the station, so they took a lift seven levels up to where the official UBU transport shuttles docked.

The cavernous terminal was filled with meandering people waiting for their shuttles to take off. Each had the same sort of disgruntled look on their face for having to take this reliable but frustrating form of public transportation. Which was good for Lyssa and Sage, because it meant these weren't part of the manhunt.

Lyssa'd never worried about anyone from the Academy recognizing her as Razia, or vice versa. But next to Sage, whose disguise was nothing more than a lab coat and handsome silver-framed glasses, more people might make that connection.

Sage seemed to share her nerves. "Keep your eyes down."

"Hey, this is my disguise," she snapped back, but without much heat. "I do this all the time—"

"Yeah, but you're wanted for a billion credits right now," Sage reminded her, "so I think people are paying just a hint more attention than usual."

As if the Great Creator was proving his point, both of their faces flashed on a nearby advertisement screen. She ducked her head down and wished she had her glasses with her.

Sage seemed to notice her heightened nerves and slipped his hand through hers, intertwining their fingers. The gesture was at once calming and not. She wondered not only when she gave Sage permission to take her hand, but when she began to like the way it felt.

Still, she didn't let go until their shuttle docked safely at the Academy.

# CHAPTER FOURTEEN

The sight of lab coats and the sterile air of the Academy of Planetary and System Science was welcome once they exited the transport shuttle. Lyssa was a little surer they wouldn't be recognized there, although she knew all too well that the U-POL could be lurking around any corner. More focused on moving cartons and specimens, rather than the two most wanted people in the universe, the scientists and dock workers ignored them. It was nice to not worry about being captured, at least for a moment.

She and Sage kept their heads down as they left transport shuttle, taking a freight elevator instead of the regular lifts down to the station where Lyssa's ship sat blissfully unguarded since Lizbeth had landed it a few hours before.

Lyssa opened the hatch and climbed on board, happy to be home. She headed straight for the bedroom to change out of the Academy student uniform and into something a bit more normal. She found her glasses on the sink where she'd left them. Sliding them on always made her feel a little bit more hidden.

When she walked out, she found Sage, deep in thought, settled on the bed.

She leaned against the doorframe of her bathroom. "I'll go get Heelin. You make sure you stay hidden when we get back, okay?"

Sage turned to look at her with a smirk. "I don't get to meet more of your brothers? I know how much you love it." When she scowled at him, he chuckled. "How many siblings do you have?"

"Twenty-three."

Sage whistled. "Busy parents."

Lyssa shifted. "Yeah well. I'm not sure they're all his." To Sage's surprised look, she added, "Don't say anything to Vel. He's kind of attached to Sostas."

"Wouldn't dream of it."

She paused, watching him lay on her bed, and the most peculiar urge to ask him to stay at the Academy station rose within her. After all, he'd be safe from Jukin and Opli and all of the other mess that she'd made.

She imagined the noose around his neck and shook the image from her head.

"Something wrong?" he asked, noticing her staring at him.

Wordlessly, she spun around and disappeared.

***

Lyssa didn't know where she'd find Heelin, but she thought she would try Dorst's lab first. He seemed to be the central meeting ground for the Peates, so if Heelin wasn't there, she'd at least have some leads to hunt him down.

*Well*, she thought ironically, *I'm finally hunting someone.*

She walked into Dorst's lab, scanning the room as she'd scan any bar on D-882. She paused on each face, her brow furrowed in—

"Well, look who it is."

She scowled and turned to the sound of the voice—Dorst's—and was more than slightly alarmed that he looked absolutely livid to see her.

But she wasn't about to let him know that. "I need to talk to Heelin."

"I can't imagine why, Lyssa, since you deliberately disobeyed a direct order from me." Dorst sounded a little too much like Sostas for comfort, but she tried to brush it off.

"Which order was that?"

"The one where you promised me you would work with Heelin!" Dorst exploded. "The one where you sat in my office and *promised* me you would do better, and then five seconds later, you walked out the damned door and disappeared again!"

"Oh yeah." She winced and realized that Dorst had no idea about Lizbeth's call or testifying or the Pirate Ball. In his eyes, she'd basically taken his earnest request and told him to shove it. And for some reason that made her feel guilty.

"Well, I'm here now, and I've…I'm here to talk to him finally."

Dorst pinched the bridge of his nose. "Whatever. Just know I'm not covering for you anymore. What do I care if they kick you out of the Academy?"

She ignored the rest of Dorst's complaining because she finally saw Heelin on the other side of the lab, peering into a microscope. Nearly running across the room, she leaned on the table next to him, plastering a nice look on her face.

"Hey Heelin."

"What do you want?" he snapped, not looking up at her.

"Just wanted to have a little chat about your career," Lyssa said, glancing at the clock on the wall and reminding herself that they had less than a day before the executions began. "Wanted to follow up on our conversation from a few weeks ago."

"The one you left in the middle of?"

She winced again; she really had screwed herself, hadn't she? "Yeah, that one. Sorry about that. I have… a lot going on right now."

"I'm sure."

She brushed off the glib remark. "As your supervisor—"

"You're not my supervisor anymore."

"As your big sister—"

"You're a year younger than me."

"*As your colleague*," she barked. "I think maybe now is the right time to…" She glanced at the time on the wall again. "Now's the time to join the U-POL."

Heelin nearly fell off his chair, his eyes wide with shock.

"How did you know about that?"

She shrugged. "Dorst?"

Heelin grumbled and she caught an under-the-breath curse word. "What's the point? Mother would never let me. Jukin would probably never let me."

"Have you ever asked?"

"No, but—"

"Well, how will you know if you never ask? Come on, call Jukin now. I'll even take you there!"

Heelin played with the pen at his side, tapping it against the notepad. Lyssa held her breath as the wheels turned in his head. He sighed in defeat.

"It'll never work."

Lyssa balled her first, unwilling to take no for an answer. "Come on, Heelin. You're miserable here. Do you really want to be unhappy for the rest of your life?"

"Why do you keep coming back?"

She furrowed her brow. "Why do I…what?"

"You've obviously found your calling, and yet you come back here every couple of weeks. I just…why?"

"That's not important." She waved him off. "We're talking about you, right?"

"But it is important. If I were to do this, it'd be a clean break. I'd have to leave the Academy for good to join the U-POL. So I guess if you haven't made a clean break…"

She shrugged. "I don't know why I keep coming back here. Maybe I just like using desolate planets as my personal training gym, or maybe I like the shitty food. But you are not me, so you'll have to make your decisions for yourself."

"But I've never done that before. Every single life choice has been made for me since I was born."

Lyssa nearly throttled him. One hundred lives hung in the balance, and her ticket into the prison was waxing poetic about his lack of autonomy.

"Then make a damned decision!" she snapped, sounding harsher than she meant to. "Call Jukin. Screw Mother. Just do it!"

"Why are you so interested in what I do with my life?" he growled, turning back to the microscope.

She sighed to buy her some time to think of a reason that wasn't the truth. "Because...because my own life choices haven't panned out so well lately."

"Yeah?"

"I was doing really well," she said, before adding with a grimace, "kind of. Then I lost it all. I mean...all of it."

Heelin glanced up at her.

"Afterward, I spent a lot of time moping around instead of demanding what was my due. I let people walk all over me and treat me like...like I didn't deserve to be respected." She remembered Dissident's sneer and they way she had practically begged Relleck to talk to Contestant. Hearing the runners treat her like a piece of meat at the Pirate Ball. "And I should have called them out on all of it. I should have demanded that they listen to me. But I let this one setback and my own...my own lack of self-respect get in the way."

"My application has been rejected five times," Heelin said quietly. "I'm not sure what I've done wrong, or if I'm just too old."

Lyssa couldn't believe the words that came out of her mouth next. "Well then, why didn't you ask Jukin for help sooner?"

"Because I don't need his help," Heelin snapped. "I should be able to do this on my own."

"Asking for help doesn't mean you aren't doing it on your own. It means you're being...smart and using your resources..." She stared off in the distance and reconsidered every time she snapped at Sage for helping her. Perhaps the pirate wasn't so wrong after all.

"But it's not about that," Heelin said, sitting back. "If this is truly what I'm supposed to be doing, it should be easier than this. It should just happen, right?"

She chewed on her lip. "It doesn't work like that though. If it's something you can't get out of your head, if it's something you think about when you wake up and when you go to sleep. If you can't picture yourself doing anything else...you'll make it work." She paused, considering her own words. "If it's truly your calling, you don't do it for anyone else. You do it for yourself. And when people tell you no, you just keep trying until they change their minds."

Heelin considered her words. "Would you call him with me?"

"Who? Jukin?" Lyssa shook her head violently. "Probably not the best idea. Jukin hates me—"

"I'll do it." Lyssa turned to see Dorst standing behind them with a proud smile on his face. "See, Lyss? I knew you had it in you. Very inspiring."

She snarled at Dorst's invasion into their private

conversation, not sure if she was more annoyed that he had listened in or that she had shared her thoughts. But Heelin sprang upright and walked up to Dorst with a nervous expression. "You aren't mad?"

Dorst shook his head and grasped Heelin's shoulder. "Heelin, I don't care if you're my assistant or the president of the damned Academy. You're my brother, and I just want you to be happy."

Lyssa shifted uncomfortably at the open affection between the two of them, but she shoved down any jealous feelings at the more pressing thought of Sage's crew in the prison. Time was definitely of the essence.

"So, shall we?"

***

"Sorry, Heelin," Dorst said, after the fifth try on Jukin's personal mini-computer. "Looks like Jukin's too busy to take our call."

Lyssa chewed on her lip nervously. "But I mean, Jukin needs help now, doesn't he? We should try again."

"I doubt anyone is able to get through to him." Dorst shook his head. "Don't worry, when all this dies down, I'll call him again."

Lyssa swallowed at Dorst's choice of words and stepped forward, typing in a number from memory.

"Lyssa, what are you doing?" Dorst asked.

"Heelin's going there today," she seethed.

Even if it meant she had to talk to the person who had wronged her even worse than Jukin.

The call barely rang before it was answered by a stuffy,

wig-adorned butler. "Mrs. Dr. Peate's telephone, who is calling?"

Lyssa swallowed every negative emotion that bubbled to the surface, knowing that what she was about to do was more important than whatever bad blood existed between them.

But that didn't mean she had to be nice to the help. "Get her."

The butler offered a hearty eye roll and loud sigh before standing up. The line remained open for a few minutes, and as they ticked by, Lyssa's heartbeat grew faster. This had to work. They had wasted too much time at this point.

But she knew these nerves weren't all about the pirates. She pulled her mini-computer from her lab coat and typed in a message.

*I'm about to beg my mother to talk to Jukin.*

A few seconds later, the reply came in.

*Me and the rest of piracy thank you profusely for your great sacrifice.*

She snorted and allowed a relieved smile to cross her face.

"Is that your friend Al?" Dorst asked from behind his desk.

"Al?" Lyssa blinked. Then she remembered Sage's alias and rolled her eyes.

"Who?" Heelin asked.

"Lyssa's got a boyfriend," Dorst snickered.

*"She does?"* came a high-pitched voice from the line.

Lyssa's blood ran cold as Mrs. Dr. Sostas Peate appeared on the screen in front of them. She looked just as Lyssa remembered her, plump with blonde hair perched atop her head. She was covered in enough make-up to make Lyssa's night at the Pirate Ball look like she had rolled out of bed. She peered down at the three of them with the superior air that demonstrated who held the power in their relationship.

Eleonora seemed to have overcome her searing distain for Lyssa in the interest of gossip. "So, Lyssandra, tell me of this man. I only suppose he's a fellow scientist at the Academy. I hope, in any case. The Great Creator only knows what type of man—"

"He is, Mother," Dorst interrupted. "I met him. Lovely guy."

Lyssa closed her eyes and counted to ten. "I don't have a boyfriend."

"Then my suspicions were correct then." Mrs. Dr. Sostas Peate fanned herself. "I suppose it makes sense, with your penchant for mannishness."

"Oh for crying out loud, I am not a lesbian either!" Lyssa huffed. "*But that is not what we're here to talk about!*"

"Then please get on with it. I have a very important session with Priest Helmsley to pray for Jukin."

"Yeah, about that..." Lyssa yanked Heelin to the forefront. "Heelin has something he wants to ask you."

"I do?"

"I swear to..." Lyssa trailed off, swallowing another mean comment. "Heelin wants to join Jukin, but Jukin's not taking our call."

"I should say not, he's quite busy."

"Exactly, and Heelin wants to go help him," Lyssa said. "That prison is overflowing, and I hear...I hear that a lot of his officers are looking for those two fugitives."

"Disgusting, filthy woman. She's the same heathen that kidnapped Vel, you know."

"Yes, I'm aware." Lyssa adjusted her glasses.

"And *why* aren't you having this conversation with Jukin?"

"Because..." Heelin looked back at Lyssa, confused.

"Because he wouldn't take our call," Lyssa said. "We figured that even a big shot like him wouldn't say no to a call from his mother." She watched as the concept played around in her mother's shellacked head.

"I guess..." She sighed dramatically. "I shall patch him in." She turned to an unseen person off screen and began waving her hand. "Help me with this,"—she waved at the screen—"thing."

As the servant puttered with the machine, Lyssa looked toward the door. She was dressed in a lab coat, her hair pulled back in a bun, her glasses on, but...there was the chance. She was one-half of the most wanted pirate duo (she allowed herself a little smile at that thought). Jukin had to make the connection.

Then again, her own mother and two of her brothers were staring right at her and hadn't.

Dorst caught her staring at him, and she quickly turned away. The screen divided as the secondary call was patched in. Two rings later, and Lyssa's heart pounded as it connected.

"Mother, I am *very* busy..." Jukin stopped, looking at the screen. It was clear that he'd gotten about as much sleep as Lyssa had in the hours since his mass arrest. He looked worn, haggard. Like a man who was barely hanging onto his victory.

Perhaps this plan would work better than expected. After all, he only numbered fifty Special Forces officers, and some of those presumably would be out looking for her. The rest of the security forces served merely because their other paychecks had dried up.

Jukin sputtered in confusion and anger at being ambushed. "What is this? Why are they here?"

"Because you wouldn't answer my call," Dorst snapped, and Lyssa was sure he would have added "asshole" if their mother hadn't been on the line.

"I'm *busy*."

"Too busy for family?"

"Yes, as a matter of fact."

Mrs. Dr. Sostas Peate cleared her throat, as if used to these brotherly squabbles. On cue, Jukin and Dorst quieted. "Heelin would like to join you there on that dreadful planet."

Jukin sighed and rubbed the stubble on his face. "Mother, I can't possibly even consider—"

Lyssa twitched and sat back, waiting for the fireworks. No one said no to Mrs. Dr. Sostas Peate.

"Excuse *me*, son?" Her voice sounded like poison, and it made Lyssa's hair stand on end. Even though she wasn't the object of the anger, it still made her uncomfortable. To her relief, Jukin seemed similarly rattled by it.

"What I meant, Mother, was that I've got my hands full here," Jukin said, pushing the words out through a pleasant filter, "and that I can't take time away from the job at hand to babysit."

Lyssa's face twitched at the casual way he spoke about executing a hundred men, but she nudged Heelin to prod him to speak.

"You won't have to babysit me," Heelin responded. "I want to be helpful."

Jukin let out a long breath, glancing between Heelin and what was presumably the visage of their mother.

"I don't even know how you would get here."

"Icanbringhim!" Lyssa blurted out, seizing the opportunity. Jukin's eyes drifted over to her, and for a brief and horrifying moment, she wondered if he recognized her. When he said nothing, she swallowed and said more slowly, "I can drop him off on my way."

"Fine." He looked at his watch and snorted. "Come the day after tomorrow—"

"NO!" That was too late, after Jukin's first round of executions. They had to go now. Everyone stared at her and she coughed. "I mean, I'm about to…do an…experiment. Time sensitive, can't wait." She swallowed and tried to look normal as she added the crushing blow, "Leveman's Vortex, you know. Planetary alignments. Important stuff. Once in a blue moon."

She watched the muscle tighten in Jukin's jaw and knew that he must think she was going to work with Sostas. As much as that delighted her, she needed him to not react emotionally.

"We'll be there in four hours," Lyssa said, standing up with all the authority she didn't feel. "Be sure to have the red carpet out for us."

***

"Quit tapping your foot so loudly," Heelin scowled.

"Sorry," Lyssa whispered, ceasing her movement and focusing on the black space in front of them.

Dorst was happy to send them off, his underlying anger at Jukin palpable underneath a cheerful veneer. He and Heelin made most of the conversation on the way back to Lyssa's ship, with Dorst agreeing not to make any changes to Heelin's employment records until Heelin was sure this was what he wanted. He also tossed in a few thinly veiled barbs at Jukin, which made Lyssa almost fond of her second eldest brother by the time they said goodbye. He also seemed to have forgiven Lyssa's disappearances, as he requested another career council session the next time she was at the Academy, and she was half-inclined to actually show up for it.

If she survived.

"I have to go check something downstairs," she said, needing to move before she dwelled on that thought anymore. "Stay…stay up here."

"Why?"

"I don't want you getting into my stuff," she said, hoping she sounded serious. When Heelin looked uninterested, she hurried down the back of the ship into the lower level. She typed the code into her bedroom door and walked in.

Sage looked comfortable, his hands behind his head and his ankles crossed. She wouldn't have guessed that he was nervous, except for the small crease in his forehead. He turned his head and smiled at her when she walked in, obviously trying to hide his concern. She wondered how often he did that around her and why she never noticed it before.

"You know, Lyss, I thought my bed was uncomfortable. How do you sleep on a rock like this?"

"It's fine," she said.

"Bouncy," he said, adjusting himself on it.

"I wouldn't know."

He sat up as she perched on the edge of the bed. "How's it going up there?"

"We should be there soon." She looked up towards the ceiling where she knew Heelin sat on her bridge. "So far, I don't think Jukin suspects a thing."

"Good."

Silence fell between them, and her own mind filled with anxious thoughts. To distract herself, she turned to Sage and said, "Heelin's a real dick though. I don't know what his problem is."

"In what way?" Sage asked with an amused tone.

"I mean..." She crossed her arms. "He's just...mean. I didn't do anything to him, and he's just..."

Sage nodded. "Doesn't appreciate anything—especially when you try to help him?"

"Yeah, and he's rude. Short and snippy."

"Quick to anger and stubborn?"

She nodded. "I just...I can barely stand to be around him for more than a minute. I feel like he's going to bite my head off."

"I think I know someone like that. Real pain in my ass."

She glared at him, catching on finally. "I'm not *that* bad."

"You're pretty bad." He paused. "Not as bad as you used

to be, but still pretty bad. So now you know how everyone else feels in your company sometimes." He lay back down and chuckled. "I should win an award for putting up with your bullshit for as long as I have."

"I'll get right on that." She glanced over at him as he settled back into his worried thoughts. In the back of her own mind, she began to wonder if it was such a good idea to bring Sage. He could be reckless and idiotic sometimes, and with his crew in the balance, she wasn't sure he wouldn't do something stupid. And if something happened to him, she'd never be able to forgive herself.

"You keep looking at me like that." Sage's voice cut through her thoughts. "What's with you?"

"Oi! Lyssa! They're calling for you!" Heelin barked from the upper level.

"C-coming!" she called, moving to stand.

"Wait."

Sage grabbed her hand and pulled her back down. He reached up his hand and cupped her cheek. Something cold and metallic slipped into her ear canal.

"Comms," he explained, tapping the device inside of her ear. A static sound buzzed in her ear. "Press it once to speak, twice to turn the speaker on and off." His voice echoed in one ear, but was delayed a millisecond in the speaker in her other ear.

"Thanks," she whispered.

"Cough twice if something goes wrong, okay?"

She nodded, wondering what Sage could do if things went wrong. And again, she wondered if she should knock him upside the head and attempt this by herself.

"*Lyssandra, they want to talk to you!*"

"Here goes nothing," Lyssa said to Sage.

His hand was still clasping hers and he squeezed it. "I'll be right in your ear."

# CHAPTER FIFTEEN

The prison was a small speck in the distance, and if she hadn't had the exact coordinates for it, Lyssa never would have found it among the rolling orange dunes of D-882. As they got closer, she spotted the massive building, tinted orange from the dust, and she noticed the cranes, the building material, and the fact that only two of the wings looked operational.

With a glance over at Heelin, she reached up to her ear discreetly and tapped the microphone once. "So, looks like the prison is still under construction. Couple of wings aren't finished."

*"What?"* Sage hissed in her ear. *"Shit, Lyssa, which ones are they?"*

"You know Jukin didn't get enough money to finish them," Heelin said as if this were common knowledge. "Only two wings are operational."

"Two wings operational, huh?"

*"Which ones, Lyss?"*

"Looks like the east wing and the southeast, right?" Lyssa said.

"I'm sure I don't care," Heelin drawled.

*"Shit, that changes things. Okay. We'll make it work, don't worry."*

"I'm not worried," she said.

"What'd you say?" Heelin asked.

"N-nothing. Just talking to myself."

Sage must not have realized he left his microphone on, because he began cursing something filthy and talking to himself. She listened to him think aloud, second-guessing himself and cursing more and it made her wonder—yet again—if she should try to keep him out of this.

The ship landed in the loading dock on the planet and Lyssa let out a long, shaky breath that she hoped neither Heelin nor Sage heard. She pushed herself out of her chair, imprinting in her mind the way the leather felt, the arrangement of the buttons on her dashboard. Even the way it smelled, a sterile sort of familiar scent.

She followed Heelin down the back ladder, taking each step slowly and deliberately. She glanced back to the closed door to her bedroom and wished she'd spent more time remembering every detail of it.

"Are you quite ready? I thought you had places to be,"

Heelin growled. She nodded and walked over to the door, pressing the button to lower her back ramp.

The smell of the desert washed over her, at once familiar and unfamiliar. In the docking station, there was one other giant ship and it was big enough to house all the pirates for an escape (if they ever got that far).

Lyssa stepped out of her ship, taking stock of the exits and doors and ventilation shafts. She and Sage would be using those to crawl through to the different hubs—

*Except there were only two hubs*, she reminded herself.

"You figure out a plan yet?" she whispered.

Sage's voice filtered through her ear, *"Not yet, but I'm working on it."*

The double doors on the other side of the room slid open and Jukin walked into the cavernous docking station, followed by Opli and another officer Lyssa didn't recognize. For a brief, terrifying moment, Lyssa worried that Jukin *had* recognized her and had come to arrest her.

But the smile that broke out on his face gave her a small respite from her near constant nerves.

"Brother!" he announced, completely ignoring Lyssa as he gripped Heelin's shoulders in brotherly affection.

She could feel Opli's eyes on her and her heart began to pound loudly. She folded her arms in a futile attempt to keep it in her chest.

"Thank you for letting me come," Heelin said, similarly nervous but for different reasons. "I want to help in any way that I can."

"And we sure need it Kasan, we sure need it," Jukin said,

completely oblivious that he had called his brother by the wrong name. "My superiors were able to round up less than fifty men to guard this prison." Lyssa tried not to smile, so much for "all available forces" that General State had promised. That meant that pirates outnumbered the U-POL by two-to-one.

"Most of my unit is out combing the area for those two pirates," Jukin continued, oblivious to Lyssa's scheming. She waited for either Jukin or Opli to look at her, but they remained focused on Heelin.

"You'll get them," Heelin said with a toothy grin. Lyssa was struck with how much he suddenly looked like Vel when he first came to intern with her. Sycophantic, overly eager. "Are you close?"

Jukin's face shifted, and he forced out a smile. "It's only a matter of time. We have one of their ships in custody, and we are in the process of finding the other one. But through some kind of loyalty or just plain ignorance, none of the pirates know what her ship even *looks* like."

Lyssa smirked at her own brilliance and resisted the urge to look at the very ship they were talking about.

Jukin, however, finally noticed her standing there. His eyes seemed to look right through her. "What are you still doing here? Don't you have Father's work to complete or something like that?"

"Yeah," Lyssa nodded, knowing Sage was still on board her ship, and if they took off now, they'd lose their chance. But she couldn't resist a barb. "You know, work that actually improves lives instead of taking them."

"Leveman's, you always have a line for everything, don't you, Lyssandra?" Jukin growled.

"Familial trait, what can I say? Must have learned it from Sostas."

The blow hit as intended and Jukin's cheeks reddened while Opli's eyes narrowed. Jukin cleared his throat loudly and forced a smile at Heelin. "Shall we? You can help me in the central headquarters."

"Sounds amazing." Heelin was nearly skipping as he followed Jukin out of the docking station.

But there was still the problem of Opli, who was staring at her in a way that did not make her comfortable.

"So…you are the elusive Lyssandra Peate."

"Yeah. I need to go work on Leveman's Vortex," she stammered, turning back to the ship. Opli's hand clamped down on her wrist.

Before she could say anything, Opli's grip relaxed, and she heard him thump to the ground.

"That may be a problem later," Sage said, tossing aside the blunt object he'd used to knock out Opli.

"That may be a problem *now*!" she hissed, looking up at the cameras on the wall. "They could see you!"

"Please, who are you talking to?" Sage scoffed. "I already scrambled them while you were all chit-chatting."

She opened her mouth and then closed it. "Oh."

"Yeah, *oh*," Sage shook his head. "Now hurry up and get changed before they start to wonder why your ship hasn't left yet."

She nodded, flying back onto her ship and changing

quickly into her boots, cargo pants, and black tank top. Just as she felt better pulling on her glasses as Lyssa, now she felt more at home in her pirate gear. Razia returned to the docking station just as Sage was handcuffing an unconscious Opli to an exposed pipe, the latter now sporting a black eye and the former's knuckles were red.

"What?" Sage shrugged. "He deserved it."

She watched Sage, and she was again overcome with the need for him to stay out of danger, where her own terrible choices wouldn't affect him.

"You keep looking at me like you'll never see me again," Sage said. "I mean, I know we're about to go on a suicide mission and all, but something is off with you right now."

"Sage, I don't think this is a good idea," she whispered, stepping back and crossing her arms.

"It's a little late to back out now, don't you think?" Sage said with an exasperated glance around the docking station.

"No not that." She shook her head. "I mean…I think you should just…stay here. I'll get everyone out."

His eyes widened in disbelief. "Are you insane? First of all —"

"I'll knock you out and leave you here."

"I would love to see you try and fight me." Sage towered over her, but she could still take him if she were motivated enough. When he approached close to her, he gently took both of her arms. "What is this about?"

"This is too dangerous for you," Lyssa repeated. "And I would just feel better if you stayed here."

"What, and you go get yourself killed? No way."

"Sage, I'm not arguing—"

"Neither am I, Lyssandra." The tone of his voice even more shocking than the use of her full name. "What has gotten into you? Why would I even think about staying here while you go and—"

"*Because I wouldn't be able to forgive myself!*" The words burst forth before she could stop them.

He blinked a few times in confusion. "W...what in Leveman's does that mean?"

"Sage, it's my fault that Jukin...these guys..." She closed her eyes. "I could have put him away, and I didn't."

"Again, I have no clue what you're talking about."

"Sage, there was more to the conspiracy that Lizbeth and I uncovered," she said, waiting for the fall-out. "Jukin was hoping to frame pirates for the assassination so he could do... what he just did...capturing everyone and...and I let him walk because..."

Sage stared at her, processing what she'd told him.

"Because...oh Leveman's, I don't know," she finished, looking away from him. "Because I'm an idiot. And now we're in this mess, and it's my fault." Tears threatened, but she forced them back. "And if something happened to you because of what I didn't do...I could never forgive myself."

"Lyssa, for the hundredth time, the only person who is at fault is *Jukin.*" Sage sounded more surprised at her than angry. "*Jukin* is the one who decided to kill Tauron. *Jukin* is the one who arrested my guys. If something happened to me, it would be *Jukin's* fault."

She cautiously peered up at him. "You don't hate me for

letting him walk? For…for all this?"

"Lyssa, in what universe could I ever hate you?" Sage exclaimed. "I…You're my best friend."

"But Ganon…you said those guys were your family."

"You're part of my family, too. Whether you like it or not." He smiled at her and she couldn't breathe. "And that means that I l…" He trailed off, clearing his throat. "I care about you."

He brushed a piece of hair back behind her ear; her skin tingled where his fingers brushed her cheek.

"Even if this all goes to shit," he whispered, "even if we fail, even if we end up…I never want you to think any of this is your fault. *You* aren't responsible for what others do, okay? Especially Jukin. He'll have to answer for what he's done one day. You did what you thought was the right thing to do in that messed up brain of yours."

Lyssa nodded, not because she believed him, but to get him to stop looking at her the way he was. But that answer wasn't good enough for Sage, because he guided her chin over so she would face him.

"Understand?"

She felt uncomfortable, alarmed, nervous, scared, and it had nothing to do with their impending assault on the prison and everything to do with the way his eyes bored into hers, the closeness of his face, and the intense feeling that welled somewhere in the pit of her soul.

"*Understand?*"

"Yes," she said.

"Okay, no more of this…what'd you call it? Mushy

stuff?" His eyes glittered in mirth when she scowled at him. "We have to focus up and break some guys out of prison. Can you handle that?"

"But only two wings are operational."

"So *you're* going to go distract them," Sage said, walking over to a ventilation shaft, "and I'm going to see if I can figure out that counter code for the distress call. That way, at least, if we can get everyone out of the cells, the guards won't be able to call for reinforcements."

She nodded, at least happy that she would be the one in danger and he wouldn't. She used her mini-computer to start her ships engines and guide it off the concrete ground and out into the open desert air. She set it to orbit the planet, hoping that none of the U-POL ships surrounding the planet would notice it.

Sage was over by a ventilation shaft opening. He jumped up to yank down the grate with a loud clatter. Razia winced at the noise and turned to look at Opli, not sure why she was worried about him when he was still knocked out.

"Ladies first," Sage said. Knowing she was too short to argue with him, she let him place his hands on her hips and lift her up into the open shaft. She struggled to push herself up and felt his hands encircle her butt.

"Hey, *hands*!" she snapped, as he nearly tossed her into the shaft. A few minutes later, his fingers clasped down on the vent edges and he pulled himself up effortlessly.

"Well?" he said, almost too big for the space. "Get going."

"Don't touch my butt again," she snapped. When she turned to start crawling towards the vent, she felt him reach out and pinch her, so she kicked out a leg and connected with his arm, his amused chuckling echoing after her.

***

Sweat dripped onto the metal casing beneath Razia's hands as she crawled, wondering if the ventilation shaft was really this long or if it just felt like it. The desert sun boiled the building, and she wondered if Jukin were simply trying to kill off the pirates with heat exhaustion.

She stopped moving when she heard voices coming through a grate. She couldn't quite hear what they were saying, so she slid closer, trying not to make a sound.

"Roger that, Habuda. All quiet in cellblock five."

She glanced through the slits, realizing she was over the main command center. From what she could tell, it was the same circular room Sage's maps depicted. Giant screens lined the wall she could see, and there was a hum of activity. She shifted slightly, spying a main chair in the center that sat unoccupied. But if she craned her head, she could hear Jukin's voice.

"I don't know what's keeping Lieutenant Opli," he was saying to Heelin, who was still following him around like a lovesick puppy. "In the meantime, you can sit here with Lieutenant Witkunas and help him watch the surveillance cameras."

They moved on, and Razia realized she needed to as well. Quietly, she pulled herself across the grate, careful to not make a sound until she was well away from the command center. She came to a fork and pulled out her mini-computer to look at the plans for the direction she was headed in. She tapped her ear.

"You okay?" she asked.

A grunt came in response. *"Would be nice if I had Sobal here to do this. I've forgotten half of what I used to know about coding."*

"That's why I don't hire people. Makes you soft," she retorted, taking the left shaft.

*"Says the universe's most loneliest person."*

She grunted and turned off the microphone, not willing to get into an argument with Sage when she was supposed to be quietly making her way to the prison. But connecting with him, even briefly, was comforting.

She spotted another grate ahead and slowed her movements. She peered down, spying a central console where five officers sat, each staring at the video monitors. She craned her head and spotted the bars, and no less than twenty men crammed into jail cell built for two. She recognized Silas Brendler, Zolet Obalone, and Flynn Sloan, all still wearing their formal attire from the Pirate Ball, but there was no sign of Sage's crew.

She backed away from the grate and tapped on the speaker in her ear.

"I'm in position."

*"Do you see my guys?"*

"They're here," she said. "All look okay."

*"Liar."*

"I'm sure they're fine," she said, wondering how everyone seemed to know when she was lying these days. She used to be better at it. "But this is supposedly half of pirates. They're crammed in there pretty thick."

*"Do you think he..."*

Razia cut him off before he could finish that thought. "No, Sage. He said he wasn't going to start those until..." Today, she finished silently. "I didn't hear anything about that in the command center." Even so, she began to squirm in anticipation. "Are you finished yet?"

*"No, Lyssandra, I am not."*

"Stop calling me by my full name."

*"Then stop asking me stupid questions."*

She sat back in the vent and wiped a bead of sweat away from her brow. She would have to be patient, she supposed, and—

She jumped as the vent rattled. For a brief moment, she worried it was gunfire, but when she heard it again, she realized someone was rapping on the exposed ventilation shaft.

"Come on out up there!"

"Sage, you're gonna have to hurry it up," she whispered.

*"I can't—"*

"Come out with your hands up!"

"Well you're going to have to try," Razia said, sliding over to the grate. She kicked it open and with a prayer to the Great Creator, she slipped out.

Her feet hit the ground and she heard fifteen weapons cock in unison at her followed by the sound of whistles and catcalls from inside the cells.

"Oi! It's the girl!"

"Whatchoo doing here, girlie?"

"Shut up in there!" The commanding U-POL officer swept to the front of the weapon gaggle, with a stern look to the pirates who were still hooting and whistling from the cells. They, at least, did not seem concerned that they were all about to be executed. But perhaps they had no idea that no one else was coming for them.

"Yes, that is a good question: what are you doing here?" The commanding officer, whose lapel bore the name Banaziak, folded his arms and peered at her curiously.

She leaned back into the console desk that she'd landed next to and tried to look unconcerned about the guns pointed at her. She counted three Special Forces officers, but the rest were simply regular police. Three zealots that might shoot her if she got too mouthy. She could handle those odds.

"Well, you know, I was just so *pissed off* that you guys had another party without me," she said, checking her nails. She saw one of the Special Forces officers raise his gun higher, and she dropped her hand. "You know, I'm starting to get a little upset that you guys keep not inviting me to your things."

"Pretty stupid of you to come here alone," Banaziak replied. He paused and then nodded. "But you aren't alone, are you?" He chuckled. "Is this some sort of pathetic rescue attempt? And I can only suppose your partner in crime sent you in alone?" He scoffed. "Not much of a gentlemen to put the lady in danger."

"This lady is more dangerous than the gentleman," Razia replied. Pretending to run her hands through her hair, she tapped the device in her ear. She hissed under her breath, "And the gentleman had better hurry his ass up because I am about to be dead."

*"Hang on. . . . "*

"I heard you have a bit of an ego," Banaziak replied, not hearing the second half of her sentence. He approached closer. "Shame to have to stick you in here with the rest of these heathens. I can't vouch for your safety."

"I'm starting to get offended at your blatant disregard for my ability to take care of myself," she snapped.

"Then how about I just kill you right here and save myself the trouble of having to learn how to regard it?" At once, she saw the guns rise.

"Sage. . . " she whispered.

*"Just a few more seconds!"*

"I don't have a few seconds!" she hissed, her eyes darting around the room.

*"Got it!"*

The lights shut off, the cell doors ground open, and suddenly the room was filled with people. Razia grabbed the closest gun she could get her hands around, yanking it from the surprised officer's grip before flipping it around and ramming the butt into the officer's chin. All around her, pirates tussled and easily overpowered the attendants, three-on-one.

"Throw 'em in the cells!" Linro Lee hollered over the melee.

The emergency lights came on a few seconds later, bathing them in light. So far, she counted half of the officers in the cells, with the rest of them putting up a valiant fight against the pirates.

Razia grinned at the scene. Then a fist connected with her jaw, sending her to the ground. She saw stars for a moment, before glancing up at the barrel of a gun. Banaziak pointed it at her, a furious gleam in his eye. She swallowed and held her breath, but then Banaziak fell over from a right hook to the jaw.

"Ganon!" Razia wasn't sure which was more surprising—seeing Ganon or the relief she felt at it. She even let him pull her into one of his bear hugs, lifting her a few inches off the ground

"Good to see you, too," he said, before peering in her ear. "I take it the boss is somewhere doing the same thing?"

"He's trying to jam the signal so Jukin can't call for help," she said, tapping her ear. "Sage, you there?"

"Classic Sage," Ganon said with a smile. "Well, I suppose I owe Sobal fifty credits. I didn't think you two would be stupid enough to try something like this."

"Still might be stupid," she said, tapping her ear again. "Sage, are you there?"

When he didn't respond, her heart began to beat faster.

"Sage!" she tried again.

To her left, she saw the doors open—the doors that *weren't supposed to open*—Jukin appeared, his face a mixture of smugness and fury, Sage behind him in handcuffs followed by as many officers as could fit inside the outer hallway.

Immediately the fighting ceased, and the pirates let go of the remaining officers who weren't in the cells. Jukin's eyes swept the room, glancing over the officers in the cells, to the pirates standing outside of the cells, to Banaziak on the floor, and finally settling on Razia in the center of the room.

"Well, well," he said softly. "This was stupid."

"You're right," she retorted, feeling the eyes of the pirates in the room move to her. "This was awfully stupid of you."

The pirates laughed, but Jukin's face was unreadable.

"You're the ones who are outnumbered," he reminded her. "And I've already called for reinforcements."

Sage's eyes met hers, and she saw him nod his head almost imperceptibly with a small smile. Sage had scrambled the signal. That, at least, was good news. Out of the corner of her eye, she saw Sobal seated at a console in the cellblock, typing away furiously while the three meatheads stood guard in front of him. Sage said the kid was smart; perhaps he could figure something out.

She just had to stall.

"Well congratulations, Jukin," she said, amused at the ripple that passed through the room at the familiar tone in which she said his name. "You've won. All the pirates are in your grasp, and you can kill every last one of us just like you've always wanted. How's it feel?"

"Better once you've shut up."

"I'm sure, I'm sure." She laughed, adrenaline pumping through her veins. "You know, I've always wondered how it would feel to cheat my way to the top. Any different?"

"What are you talking about?"

"That five billion dollars you stole," she said. "You used that money to pay McDougall to kill Tauron. You used it to try and assassinate the president a few months ago. And *then*, you were going to blame these fine gentlemen for it." Another ripple through the room and she feigned surprise. "Oh yeah, that's right. Nobody knows about that but us…and now a hundred of our closest friends. Do you know how badly pirates gossip?"

"Too bad there's no one around to care as you'll all be dead soon," Jukin said, his voice scarily calm. She hadn't even scratched him. "Are you quite finished with your yammering, or shall I save us all the trouble and kill you now?"

Sage's eyes connected with hers, and she could almost read his thoughts. Sobal was still working, and she needed to buy more time.

She turned back to Jukin who wore a smug smile. He thought she had nothing left to use against him. But he was wrong; she had one final trump card. "Just tell me one thing. Do you think he'd be proud of you after all this?"

"Who?"

She closed her eyes and opened them again, steeling herself for whatever outcome this might bring. "Sostas."

"What did you say?" Jukin's entire face shifted, and she knew she'd struck gold.

"I asked you if you thought Sostas would be proud of you," she repeated, folding her arms over her chest. "Capturing all the pirates, being the big hero. Is that what this was all about? Trying to make him come back and,"—she grinned maliciously—"notice you?"

Jukin's face was controlled rage. "What in Leveman's do you know about my father?"

"That's why you joined the U-POL, isn't it? Why you dropped out of the Academy after he didn't *choose* you."

"I joined the U-POL because of you pieces of shit," Jukin growled at her. "Stealing and plundering without any consequence, threatening my family. You think you can just get away with all you've done?"

"Don't lie," Razia snarled. "This, all of this, is you trying for—"

"*My father was a piece of shit*," Jukin growled. "The day he left was a day I celebrated."

Her mouth fell open as she realized he wasn't lying. "So...you really think...all of this...is right?"

"Piracy is disgusting," Jukin said. "And every single one of you deserve to burn in Plethegon."

"And it's your job to send us there? Death is an appropriate response to hijacking transports and bounty hunting? You think Tauron's death was justified?"

"*Tauron Ball deserved what he got*."

Her world tilted. All of this time, she'd been excusing Jukin's behavior, hoping he was redeemable so it would be easier for *her* to stomach. She had been holding onto guilt for so long that it had skewed her perception of him. But for the first time, she really listened to what he was saying and it made her sick.

He wasn't some long-suffering, never-loved child. He was a monster, a murderous, evil creature. And it had nothing to do with Sostas or her—his actions were all his own. He considered himself the judge and jury of men, that he knew better than everyone else.

He had known what he was doing when he allied himself with men who would kill a president to make money.

He had known what he was doing when he killed Tauron.

He had known what he was doing when he left her on that pirate ship.

Like a dam breaking, fury erupted within her.

"Tauron Ball was ten times the man you are," she hissed. How could she have ever excused *murder*? Especially of someone that had meant so much to her? "At least he knew the difference between right and wrong. And what you're doing here is *wrong*."

Jukin pointed his gun at the space between her eyes. "Then be sure to tell him when you see him next."

She suddenly began to laugh, the irony of the situation so deliciously disturbing. She'd been there before, except it was Tauron holding a gun against her head. The moment Jukin gave Tauron the go-ahead to pull the trigger, he set in motion a chain reaction of events that led the two of them to where they stood presently. She, a pirate, he, a pirate killer.

"What's so funny?" Jukin sneered.

"You really don't see it, do you?" she whispered.

Jukin's face shifted, but it was in confusion, not realization. Then it twisted into loathing. "Shut your mouth, pirate, so I can kill you once and for all."

She raised her eyes to look into his, wanting him to see her fully before he ended her miserable life.

"Really?" She prayed that realization would dawn."You want to kill *me*?"

Maybe she could watch his face and relish in his horror of knowing his own flesh and blood was a member of the pirate webs as she lay there dead in front of him, knowing that it was his decision that led her to it.

"Go ahead."

Maybe she could carry that memory with her when her soul returned to Leveman's Vortex.

"*Be. My. Guest.*"

The world went dark.

# CHAPTER SIXTEEN

The first thing Razia noticed was that she was not, in fact, dead. And she'd suffered no bullet wounds, there was no searing pain of having her flesh torn asunder. She was still standing; she was still breathing.

The next thing she understood was that the lights had gone out in this section of the prison.

And Jukin was still mere inches from her.

She screamed and she lunged in his direction, her shoulder connecting with his chest as they tumbled to the ground. His gun went off, a bright flash in the darkness and she heard someone screaming in the distance. But they crashed to the ground and it clattered away.

She punched and clawed and kicked at him, releasing

twenty-two years of pent-up frustration as she beat at him. He pushed her back, and she landed hard on something under her arm. Her fingers clasped around the metal—his gun—and she cocked and pointed it at the dark figure.

The emergency lights came on, bathing the room in red.

Razia was on her knees, the gun focused on Jukin, whose lip was bleeding and shirt was torn. He seemed to be waiting for the inevitable.

Around her, the pirates had also taken advantage of their numbers and the lack of lights. Many of the regular officers were laying on the floor with their hands on their heads in surrender. The few Special Forces officers, still fighting the good fight though outnumbered, stopped when they spotted their leader on the ground with a gun in his face.

"Get 'em into the cells!" Sage cried, appearing in front of her, "or else Captain Peate's a goner."

"Go ahead and kill me," Jukin said, puffing his chest out. "I am ready to die for my cause."

Razia's grip tightened on the gun, and for a brief moment, she considered pulling the trigger. After all, Jukin deserved to die. He'd killed Tauron, taken a life for no reason other than it fit his own definition of justice. And he'd left her for dead. She had every right to kill him where he lay.

"What's wrong? Don't have the stomach for it?" Jukin's voice had a hint of crazed desperation.

"On the contrary," she whispered. "The easy thing to do would be to kill you. The easy way out would be to wipe your sorry ass out of the universe and send you back to the Great Creator to answer for your crimes. And believe me, I'm well aware of what's in store for you. And it's a lot more...fiery than Helmsley would let you believe."

"I have nothing to answer for—"

"*You have everything to answer for,*" she growled, digging the gun into his face. She took a shaky breath and tried to calm herself down. "But I'm not going to be the one to make you pay. You deserve to be hung out to dry, the laughing stock of the police force. After this, they won't put you in charge of sweeping floors. You'll be ruined, you'll be destroyed. And I want you to know that I don't care anymore."

He glanced up at her.

"I'm not going to blame myself for anything you do anymore. I'm not going to give you a free pass because Sostas didn't choose you. I'm not going to—"

"What in Leveman's Great Vortex are you babbling about, pirate?"

Her blood ran cold. She'd thought for sure...after all of that...he would know. He would see her for who she was. She'd given him everything, everything she'd ever held in about their father, everything she'd ever felt about him. She'd laid it all out on the table, but it was pointless, because he thought she was Razia. A space pirate bounty hunter who took his brother some time a few years ago. A blip on his radar. That's all she was to him.

It was impossible, she cursed to herself. He had to know. She'd dropped Heelin off not an hour before, he had looked right at her—

Through her. He had looked right through her. Because

Lyssa Peate didn't matter to Jukin. She hadn't mattered at eleven, and she didn't matter now.

And damn it all, she still wanted to.

A spasm of rage coursed through her and she punched Jukin unconscious, continuing to sit on top of him. She felt a hand on her shoulder, Sage's, and he pulled her to stand as Ganon and Nalton dragged Jukin's limp body towards an open cell where other officers in various stages of consciousness lay.

"Razia, my girl!" Dissident's froggy voice was in her ear. "You are spectacular. I could not be more proud to have you in my web. Off probation and free dues for a year!"

"Raz, you are an idiot!" Harms stood on the other side of her. "I couldn't believe you, standing up to Jukin. You're insane—I'm so glad you're okay. What were you thinking?"

"Are you all right?" Sage was in front of her. And his face, the concern and the knowing of what she had just gone through, was too much for her to handle.

Razia spun on her heel, not caring whom or what she ran into, and headed back toward the docking station. She needed to be alone, to find some silent planet where she could scream and rage and fury at all of life's unfairness.

When she heard footsteps behind her, she broke into a run, calling her ship down from the atmosphere as fast as it could go. The footsteps followed her, and she ran faster, as fast as when the U-POL were chasing her.

She burst into the docking station, where Opli remained unconscious and handcuffed to the wall. She flew out through the doors into the blinding sun, the heat and the wind feeling good against her skin. She needed distraction, she needed something to take her mind off of what had just happened.

Her ship landed in front of her, and she trudged through the shifting orange sand toward it, hearing voices and someone calling after her. She didn't want people. She wanted to fall apart in the privacy of her ship, the same way she had when her own mother wished she was dead. She didn't cry, but she grieved in her own way.

She climbed onto her ship, rushing up the ladder as quickly as possible so she could get off the planet. On repeat, she told herself she needed to escape, she needed to get out. Be alone. She was always alone. She wanted to be alone.

But she wasn't alone. Someone had followed her onto her ship. Gentle hands slid over hers removing them from the dashboard, and spun her around to look into green eyes tinted with worry and concern. Sage was speaking to her.

"Lyss, talk to me. Are you okay?"

She stood there, stripped to her core, unable to hide all that she was feeling. His hands slipped from hers to the small of her back and the side of her face.

"What you said to him…that must have been…"

"Please don't," she whispered, looking up at him. "I don't want to talk about it."

"Then let's talk about you never putting yourself in front of Jukin's gun again, okay?" He stared into her eyes and she prayed she could keep her composure. His hand slid across her cheek, tenderly lifting her chin. "Because I can't lose you either."

His lips brushed against hers as light as a feather. It was

tentative and foreign, a piece of him she'd never experienced before. As soon as it began, it ended, and she felt his warm breath on her face, could have sworn she heard his heart pounding. She had a new taste on her lips, his taste. It was very distracting.

And she needed a distraction right now.

Grabbing him by the shirt, she pulled him back down, crashing his lips on top of hers. She kissed him frantically, in desperate need to feel something good, anything to keep her from reality. His mouth opened on top of hers and innocence quickly turned into fiery passion as his tongue slid across hers. He pushed her back until her back hit a wall, and he pressed himself against her, so she could feel all of him.

His hands pushed hers above her head. Somewhere in the back of her throat, a moan escaped. His lips left hers, traveling the length of her neck, and she closed her eyes to the sensation of biting and sucking. His hands left hers and slid down her sides, as hers tangled in his hair.

His fingers slipped under her shirt, and up her sides until they reached the strap of her bra. But they stopped there, teasing her with the hesitation. She pushed him back a few inches, smirking at him as she took matters into her own hands and ripped off her shirt. She caught the ghost of an animalistic grin as he returned to her, and somehow his shirt disappeared as well.

Skin on skin, she wanted the rest of the clothing to come off. If they stopped, she would have to return to reality, and she wasn't ready to do that. From what was pressing against her, she was pretty sure he didn't want to stop either.

She pushed him backwards, down on her chair. He looked up at her in wonder as she climbed on top of him, and covered his mouth again with hers. But they didn't stay on the chair for long, as his hands hooked under her knees and he lifted her up, placing her on her dashboard. His mouth left hers again, traveling down her neck, to her chest. She unclasped her bra and let him take her in his mouth, clenching her fingers in his hair as he toyed with her.

She now was fairly sure that if she didn't lose the bottom half of her clothes, she was going to die. She reached down and began fiddling with his pants, when his hands stopped her.

"Wait—"

"Shut up," she whispered, grabbing the back of his head and kissing him again. She felt around at his belt, loosening the buttons and the zipper, before reaching inside and encircling the bulge that had been teasing her. He reacted immediately, moaning and leaning into her.

"Lyss," he whispered. "I don't...are you..."

"I said no talking."

"But—"

She stroked him, effectively silencing him. He finally unbuttoned and unzipped her pants, sliding them down her legs, placing a shiver-inducing kiss on the inside of her thigh as he removed them and her boots. He rejoined her, covering his mouth with hers as they now lay without any barriers between them. Her heart raced in anticipation, but again, he hesitated.

"I need to hear you tell me this is okay."

She rolled her eyes and grabbed him, guiding him inside of her. They let out a breath together, the joining strange and new and exciting. He kissed her gently and pressed his head to hers, moving his hips against hers. It was tight, but the more he moved, the better it felt. She wrapped her legs around him, and he moved faster. There was nothing else this feeling, nothing else but the need to replace every bad emotion with the euphoric feeling of…

She cried out as she released into the waves of pleasure, and smiled when he did so a few moments later. He leaned into her, his cheeks flushed and his eyes wide with the aftermath. After a moment, he buried his face in her neck, his ragged breath warming the sensitive space at her collarbone.

"Lyss…that was…" Sage whispered against her skin, placing a gently kiss where her neck met her shoulder.

Her eyes bolted open as reality crashed on top of her.

She pushed him off of her and stared at his naked body, still erect and tense. Her eyes moved up to his bare chest and his face, his mouth that was red and swollen. But his eyes were focused on her with some kind of emotion she'd never seen in them before.

It terrified her.

"Lyss?"

"This was a mistake," she whispered, finding her underwear and bra where they'd been thrown while they *had sex.*

Oh Leveman's, she just *had sex* with Sage.

*Sage.*

*SAGE.*

"Lyssa, calm down." He sounded perfectly normal, and it caused her more panic.

What had she been thinking?

She hadn't been thinking, that was for sure. If she'd been thinking, she never would have had sex with Sage Teon.

She was having trouble lacing up her boots, her hands shaking. His hands covered hers and pulled her upright, pressing her against him.

"Lyss?" He pulled back and cupped her face. That was how this all started, wasn't it? His hand on her cheek, a kiss. "Talk to me."

Tears threatened to fall, but years of training kept them firmly inside where they belonged. She couldn't look at him in the eyes, preferring to stare at his cheeks. She was afraid of seeing that strange emotion in them again.

"Lyssa."

With great pain, she raised her eyes to look into his and saw nothing but concern in them. That was a familiar look, one that wasn't as scary as the one she'd seen before.

"Speak to me," he whispered, and she heard the tiniest bit of fear in his voice. "Please...say something."

She opened her mouth to speak, but no sound came out. She couldn't figure out what to say to him, she couldn't even figure out what to think. After an eternity, words came from some part of her that wasn't in complete shock. "So, that was interesting."

Sage's countenance relaxed completely and he sighed, leaning his head into her shoulder. "God in Leveman's, Lyssa, you scared me."

"It's been a rough day." She laughed, finding some piece of her old self. She became aware that he was still completely naked, and the feel of his skin against hers reignited her desire for him. He was suddenly new and different, and she liked it very much.

"I should have stopped. I'm sorry," he whispered, pressing his forehead to hers.

She closed the space between them, the act now as familiar as breathing, but he pulled away.

"No, not until I know you're in your right mind."

"Obviously, I'm not," she scoffed, sitting back. "Or else I wouldn't have just…done that with you."

He stepped away from her, his face unreadable. Mechanically, he began picking up his clothes from where they'd been scattered around her bridge.

"Sage."

He paused mid-button on his pants and then continued, his brows furrowed. "You're right. This was a mistake."

"No kidding." Lyssa picked up her shirt and slipped it over her head. She looked at the dashboard, eyeing the fingerprints that now marred the surface where she had clutched and clawed at it. The rush was still present in the forefront of her mind, as was the new knowledge of the entirety of Sage's body. "But it was kind of fun."

He stopped again, cocking his head at her. "It was."

The urge to ask him to stay was strong inside of her, but the counter-urge to keep quiet was stronger. The tug-of-war was a boisterous soundtrack while she watched him finish dressing.

"You don't regret it, do you?" he asked, lacing up his shoes.

She was silent for a long time. He was almost out of her bridge before she answered.

"No."

He paused, a sly grin curling on his face.

# CHAPTER SEVENTEEN

| | |
|---|---|
|  | 1) (No last name listed), Razia |
| Wanted for | Engagement in piracy, bounty hunting, kidnapping, aggravated assault, resisting arrest, jailbreak, attempted murder of a police officer |
| Reward | 101,548,965C |
| Known Alias | None |
| Known Accomplices | Tauron Ball, Sage Teon |
| Pirate Web Affiliation | Dissident |

"It's beautiful, isn't it?"

"Yes, honey," Lizbeth said, her voice coming through Lyssa's mini-computer though the screen reflected Razia's bounty poster. "You are the most wanted pirate in the whole damned universe. Congratulations."

Lyssa grinned, glancing about the Academy transport shuttle terminal to make sure no one had heard the overzealous government investigator. After a breath, Lyssa switched the mini-computer application back to Lizbeth. "Harms said the bounties are mostly temporary. The other pirates' way of saying thank you. I'm sure it'll be gone within a week or so."

"All of it?"

Lyssa grinned. "No."

It had been three weeks since the mass riot and breakout at the prison. It was highly embarrassing for the entire U-POL. Lyssa was happy to note that General State's approval ratings tanked, especially when he seemingly flip-flopped on the issue at a recent press conference.

"See? I was right. Going to the Pirate Ball was a good idea," Lizbeth said before adding, "*eventually.*"

"Yeah, and it was a lot of bullshit to wade through before it was *eventually* all right."

"You are never satisfied, are you?" Lizbeth said, shaking her head.

Lyssa grinned.

"You know, it's funny. If none of this pirate jail stuff had happened, no one ever would have known about his involvement with the assassination," Lizbeth said, laying back on the deck chair and pulling on her sunglasses. The lake was visible behind her, as was Joe puttering on his boat. "At least, Harman and Jos never mentioned him in their interviews.

But now that you amended your testimony, they're all kinds of chatty, eager to drag him down so they don't fry as badly. Jukin is sunk no matter what he does."

Lyssa hated that she still felt guilty. "What are they going to do to him?"

"Depends," Lizbeth said. "The prosecutor's main focus is Harman and Jos, so if Jukin gives him something to work with, he might just get a slap on the hand. Jukin just looks like a guy who saw an opportunity to advance his own agenda. I don't genuinely believe that he wanted Llendo dead and without proof of that, he's just looking at a conspiracy charge." She sighed and took a long sip of her drink, shifting in the sunlight. "But his trial isn't for another year, at least. Lucky your family has all that money to bail him out."

Lyssa snorted. "I doubt Jukin's in a state to do anything. Dorst said he hasn't left his room in weeks."

"Well, it looks like you won, huh?"

Lyssa shifted. "What do you mean?"

"Jukin's effectively out of power, for good this time, and all the pirates love you." She tilted her sunglasses down to smirk at Lyssa. "And, of course, you and Sage finally got together."

Lyssa nearly choked on her spit and dropped her mini-computer. "We are *not* together."

"Maybe you think that," Lizbeth muttered, before adding. "How many times have you seen him in the past week?"

Lyssa clammed up, not wanting to tell Lizbeth that a few hours ago Sage had shown up at the Academy in that ridiculous scientist get up he had. Before that, a hurried make-out session turned had into an all night tryst at a motel. And before that…

It was a compulsion now, and she hated it. She had never seen Sage so often, and every time she spotted him, all she could think about was the feel of his body against hers, the sight of him completely naked. The way he looked at her like he was going to devour her whole. She wasn't sure if she wanted this, but she was enjoying herself regardless.

"Hello, Lyssa? Are you still here?" Lizbeth asked.

"Yes, what?" she snapped, unhappy that Lizbeth had caught her daydreaming about Sage, and unhappy that she was now turned on and Sage was on his way back to his ship on G-249.

"So when's the wedding?"

"No, no, no." Lyssa shook her head. "It's just…we're just fooling around. It's not…we're not…"

"Madly in love?"

"I want to make it absolutely, unequivocally clear that we are not…that."

"Yeah okay," Lizbeth said with an obvious disbelief that Lyssa glared at her for. "So since you're the most wanted person in the universe, I take it you're hiding out at the Academy?"

"Kind of," she said, grinning as the transport shuttle screen changed in front of her. "Vel gets back today."

"Oh yeah, I forgot about him," Lizbeth said thoughtfully. "Boy, you're going to have to take some time catching him up on all the latest. I'm sure he'll be happy that you and Sage—"

Lyssa ended the call before Lizbeth could continue talking about it. Lyssa glowered at the blank screen, hoping that Lizbeth felt her ire.

But Lizbeth had been correct. Lyssa finally had everything she wanted. She had a healthy number of bounties—real bounties, even—on her head. She hadn't chanced it on D-882 yet, but from what Harms had said, everyone was impressed with the way she had fearlessly confronted Jukin.

Except they didn't know the whole story. To them, Razia was sticking it to Jukin, but to Lyssa, laying it out to Jukin and *not* having him know the truth was killing her inside.

"Hey, Lyss."

Lyssa ignored the blond young man in front of her, and then did a double take. He certainly looked like Vel, but this man was tall, muscular, tan, and sprouted something of a curly beard that patched over his face. He looked ten years older than the last time she saw him, like he'd completed puberty in three short months.

"Hey…" She almost called him "kiddo" but the name didn't seem to fit anymore. He dropped his bag and rushed over to wrap his arms around her. She gagged at his odor, but let him tower over her.

"Did you get shorter?" he asked, looking down at her.

"You smell terrible."

"Well, sorry," Vel said, easily picking up his bags. "I just spent three months on a planet *alone*."

The emphasis caught her attention. "I thought you didn't want me to come get you!"

"I thought you would at least visit."

"Sorry, I've been a little busy trying to save the system of piracy,"—she poked him in the chest—"again."

"What happened?" Vel asked.

"I...will explain later," Lyssa said, spotting another person walking off of another shuttle on the other side of the large terminal. She locked eyes with him, but couldn't hide behind Vel's broad shoulders quick enough.

"*You*!"

She winced as Heelin's voice echoed across the transport station.

"*You did this*!"

"I did what?" She couldn't breathe. Did he recognize her? Did he see her wanted poster and realize that Lyssa Peate was really Razia?

"I was locked in a prison for days because of you!" Heelin bellowed. "*You and your stupid career advice!*"

Lyssa blinked. "What?"

"That was your plan all along, wasn't it? You and Dorst, showing me what life was like outside of the Academy, huh? Well you know it worked! I never want to be anything other than a stupid Doctor of Close Space Exploration—"

"Hang on," Lyssa blinked. "You're a CSE?"

"Yes, of course," Heelin said. "Don't you remember after our sixth year, I stopped...."

Lyssa shrugged and glanced at Vel, who was shaking his head.

"You know what, *fine*! I'm happy being here. I'm happy working for Dorst. At least that way, the only thing I have to worry about is whether or not he leaves me on a planet!"

And with that, Heelin stormed off in a very familiar way.

"Do I really act like that?" Lyssa asked Vel.

"Oh Leveman's, you're a thousand times worse," Vel said with a laugh. "You really didn't know he was a CSE? You had three months to get to know him."

"I was busy!" Lyssa snapped. "Again, saving the system of piracy as we..." Her gaze landed on the other person who had exited the transport shuttle. Opli stared back at her with a cool sort of observation, a sly smile on his face. She swallowed her fear and forced herself to look indifferent, the way that Lyssa would look at a police officer. And she just hoped that's whom he saw as he stalked over to them.

"H-hey," she said to Vel, who immediately noticed the change in demeanor. "Why don't you go grab a shower and I'll take you to lunch, huh?"

"S-sure?" Vel said. "You okay?"

Lyssa locked eyes with Opli as he approached and forced a smile on her face. "I don't know yet."

"Well, well, well," Opli said. "I admit, I'm a little surprised to see you here."

"Lyss?" Vel asked.

"Scram, kid," Lyssa barked to Vel. For a brief moment, she could see him considering whether to stay, but thankfully he turned to walk away, glancing back at them once or twice before leaving the terminal.

"This answers so many questions I have about you," Opli said, "namely, what you were doing here a year ago."

"You'll have to be more specific."

"Don't play games, pirate." A cold dread took hold of her.

He knew. "Tell me: do you take me for an idiot?"

"You do work for my brother." She paused with a very Razia-like grin. "Well, used to."

"And yet, as much trouble as you've given us, he doesn't recognize you," Opli sneered. "That says more about Lyssandra Peate than Razia, doesn't it?"

"I actually don't think that's any of your business, unless you're now part of the family. Did I miss the wedding announcement?"

"You obviously missed the press announcement promoting me to Captain of the Special Forces." Opli leaned in closer and Lyssa saw the new patch on his chest. Something about that unnerved her.

"And I guess you'll have as much success as your predecessor," Lyssa retorted. "No one is ever going to let you pull something like that again. The runners have made sure of it."

"Do you know what your brother's problem was? He believed his own words too much. He thought if he simply proved how right he was, people would suddenly respect him."

She didn't like how uncomfortably close that description was to her own troubles with bounty hunting. "And you don't?"

"I like to take precautions before I make my move. Wait for the opportune moment to strike."

She mirrored his expression. "And I can only guess that you'll be waiting for the opportune moment to share my little secret, hm?"

"Right now, it suits me to keep that nugget of information to myself," Opli said and that made her more nervous. "You may think that you're safe, but you are far from it." He paused and looked in the direction that Vel had walked off. "And so is everyone you care about."

And with that, he turned to saunter away, leaving Lyssa to ponder what kind of man she was now dealing with.

Lyssa's story continues in

# FUSION

Available Now

# ALSO BY THE AUTHOR

## The Lexie Carrigan Chronicles

Lexie Carrigan thought she was weird enough until her family drops a bomb on her—she's magical. Now the girl who's never made waves is blowing up her nightstand and no one seems to want to help her. That is, until a kind gentleman shows up with all the answers. But Lexie finds out being magical is the least weird thing about her.

Spells and Sorcery is the first book in the Lexie Carrigan Chronicles, and is available now in eBook, Paperback, Audiobook, and Hardcover.

## Demon Spring Trilogy

Three years ago, Jack Grenard's wife was brutally murdered by demons. Now, along with his partner Cam Macarro, he's trying to rebuild his life in Atlanta. But on a routine investigation, they find a demon who saves instead of kills. They must discover who she is before Demon Spring, the quadrennial breach between the human world and demon realm, when all hell—literally—breaks loose.

The Demon Spring Trilogy is the first urban fantasy from S. Usher Evans and will be released in 2018 in eBook, Paperback, and Hardcover.

# ALSO BY THE AUTHOR

## empath

Lauren Dailey is in break-up hell, but if you ask her she's doing just great. She hears a mysterious voice promising an easy escape from her problems and finds herself in a brand new world where she has the power to feel what others are feeling. Just one problem—there's a dragon in the mountains that happens to eat Empaths. And it might be the source of the mysterious voice tempting her deeper into her own darkness.

Empath is a stand-alone fantasy that is available now in eBook, Paperback, and Hardcover.

## The Madion War Trilogy

He's a prince, she's a pilot, they're at war. But when they are marooned on a deserted island hundreds of miles from either nation, they must set aside their differences and work together if they want to survive.

The Madion War Trilogy is available in eBook, paperback, and hardcover. Download the first book, The Island, for free on all eBookstores.

# ACKNOWLEDGEMENTS

As always, thank you, dear reader, for going with me on this adventure. As an indie author, I rely on my awesome folks like yourselves to help share the word about my work. Please consider leaving a review on Amazon, Goodreads, or any other fine book retailer. I am so excited to hear what you think—even if it's a short review. And don't forget to check out my other work below and subscribe to my newsletter to get all the latest info from yours truly.

To the betas, Bex, Kristin, Julia, Christina, Kat: thank you for calming my nervous brain and helping me get this book reader-ready. I love that you all know Razia as much as I do, and continue to read about her with such enthusiasm.

To Gina, you are a Godsend. Never would I have imagined I'd get so much joy in seeing all of my horrible mistakes in line edits.

To Mom and Dad, thanks for putting up with my bullshit this year. You know what I mean.

# ABØUT THE AUTHØR

S. Usher Evans was born and raised in Pensacola, Florida. After a decade of fighting bureaucratic battles as an IT consultant in Washington, DC, she suffered a massive quarter-life-crisis. She decided fighting dragons was more fun than writing policy, so she moved back to Pensacola to write books full-time. She currently resides with her two dogs, Zoe and Mr. Biscuit, and frequently can be found plotting on the beach.


Visit S. Usher Evans online at:
http://www.susherevans.com/

Twitter: www.twitter.com/susherevans
Facebook: www.facebook.com/susherevans
Instagram: www.instagram.com/susherevans

CPSIA information can be obtained
at www.ICGtesting.com
Printed in the USA
BVHW091827111121
621197BV00013B/1058/J

9 781945 438011